The Listener

THE
LISTENER

John Gill

STEIN AND DAY/*Publishers*/New York

First published in the United States in 1972 by Stein and Day/*Publishers*
Copyright © 1972 by John Gill
Library of Congress Catalog Card No. 70–187520
All rights reserved
Designed by David Miller
Printed in the United States of America
Stein and Day/*Publishers*/7 East 48 Street, New York, N.Y. 10017
ISBN 0–8128–1475–4

For Pepi

La scandale du monde est ce qui fait l'offense,
Et ce n'est pas pécher que pécher en silence

Molière

The Listener

PART
I

[1]

It was dusk when Denis Fleming parked his car in the Market Square.

As he crossed the cobbled square, his steps echoed sharply off the Gothic front of the Guild Hall. He glanced up at the window of his office, which was above his store, and wondered whether there would be a message on his desk from Louise.

The shopfront was brightly lit. Several television screens showed a newscaster talking earnestly, and in front of them a wall spit was turning slowly, a dramatic kaleidoscope of hellfire

.

The spit was the centerpiece of the window display, with plastic kabobs and broilers revolving in the glare. The sound, which was just audible in the street, was a refinement Denis had added himself—a continuous belt of tape running through a concealed amplifier which produced the authentic hiss and crackle of a barbecue. People were always stopping to look and listen, and Denis prided himself on the *réalité*.

The gold lettering on the door said "Fleming & Company, Television & Electrical Engineers." He unlocked it and went in. The company was a private one, since the only other partner was Louise. A sleeping partner, the accountant always said, with unwearying innuendo.

He crossed the showroom, walked through the empty workshop where the benches were littered with the skeletons of television sets, and went upstairs to his private office. As he turned on the desk lamp he saw that the pad was empty.

There was no message.

It was a week since he'd advertised the cottage in the London *Evening News* and daily he expected Louise to call to say she'd rented it to someone. But although quite a lot of people had telephoned, none of them had been entirely suitable. It wasn't really a good place for children and they both agreed a bachelor was ideal. And there were rather special qualifications, he thought sadly.

He pressed the bristle of his moustache lightly with his forefinger, trying to stop the onrush of thoughts, as a man might try and stop a sneeze. It was a frequent mannerism, one of which Louise complained. Then his head jerked and his face contracted as a sudden blast rattled the windows.

A pair of Phantoms, the last flight of the day, sank over the rooftops, making for the U.S. air base at Bentwaters. He moved to the window in time to see their navigation lights dimming in the dusk before they dropped out of sight. He looked down into the square. Except for his own car it was empty. On the opposite side a dark girl was locking the stable-type door of Teen Scene, the children's boutique. Denis turned away and went to the bottom drawer of his desk, lifting out a glass and bottle. He poured himself a large measure of malt whisky. He moved back and his hand rested for a moment on the tape deck. It was the hour of his private indulgence. He always tried to think of it in these terms . . . and not as a perversion or anything twisted like that.

He reached up to draw the curtains at last.

After he'd threaded the tape he ran it off at top speed until he heard the high-pitched clack of voices, then he stopped it and pressed the normal playback button. He heard first the scrape of fabric and then a small moan of contentment, before Louise said, "Put my glass down, darling." It was followed by a long exhalation of breath.

Denis Fleming knew from experience that his wife had begun to make love.

He moved away, still carrying his glass and thinking about the cottage again. The advertisement in the London *Evening News* was really the key to the future, which was why it was important to get exactly the right tenant. He needed to exercise the same care a criminal might exercise in selecting some anonymous victim. But he was not really a criminal and the new tenant, whoever he was, would not knowingly be victimized.

Suddenly from the speaker a man's voice whispered, "Oh God . . ." with a kind of agonized fervor, but though he waited motionless nothing more was said; there was only the sound of their breathing. The sound quality was not particularly good, he thought fleetingly, and already he sensed that today was not to be an exceptional occasion.

The springs creaked as they changed position and then Louise was murmuring, "Super . . . darling. Super. . . ."

Denis closed his eyes. What awful banalities made up the language of love. He took a sip of whisky and held it tingling in his mouth. The sounds of movement seemed to go on for ages. Once she said sharply, "No, darling!" She was always the dominant partner, giving instructions as precisely as a general conducting an operation of war. The thought was lost in her sudden gasp of pain. "You're hurting. . . ." Then the chaise was shifting slightly on its legs, creaking against the parquet.

"Oh no. . . ." She said it loudly, several times over, and suddenly the speaker was alive with their half-stifled cries and countercries. Denis knew that she was near her climax. The man began to groan and a moment later came her wild cry. It was as always a sustained, liturgical sound, half sung, half spoken, like a long Amen. Then there was only the rasp of their breathing.

Denis bent to the open drawer and brought out the whisky bottle. What excited her was aggression, he thought calmly. She demanded a contest, a challenge to her authority, the simulation of a fight. In a peculiar way hate had to ritualize itself in the act of love. He sipped his drink and carried it across to the window, parting the curtains with a finger.

In the illuminated window of Teen Scene, a gangly lion was waving its puppet paw at the empty square. Denis watched it, waiting. Soon there would be the inevitable post-coital conversation. That was another curious thing—

the way lovers had the same compulsion to talk afterward as men who had been in battle. After the draining of the body, the draining of the soul. But today even this was denied him, for after only a minute or two her bare feet were squeaking away on the wooden floor.

"You don't mind if I hurry you off today, but I've got to go into town." When the lovemaking was done she still gave the orders, he thought.

He moved to the tape deck and punched the reverse-wind button. He had been right, it was an unexceptional day, not worth the space in his precious library. He went back to the desk, put his glass away in the bottom drawer, and closed it. Then he turned off the desk lamp.

He stood by the door for a moment, feeling an odd lassitude. He had long ago analyzed his condition, so long ago that he rarely thought objectively about it now. He was a kind of *voyeur*, he supposed, except that his vicarious pleasure lay in the sounds of love.

An *écouteur* . . . that was what he really was. Standing there in the darkened room he repeated it. "I am an *écouteur*." He said it loudly, without pride.

Corder had been told to get the train from Liverpool Street Station.

It was as busy as an anthill and although he was half a head taller than anyone else he had to push his way around with difficulty before he found the right platform. He got into a compartment where there were already an elderly couple and a minister of the church. The minister said, "Good morning," in a resonant voice.

Thereafter there was a thoroughly British silence. Each time he raised his eyes, the eyes of the others, as sensitive as sea anemones, would be closing or moving somewhere else. They were isolated in a way by their propinquity. Corder stirred restively.

He had stopped by the American Consulate in Belgrave Square to pick up his mail and he opened it up as the train rattled away through the London haze. There were two handouts from a technical publisher which the University had sent on and which advertised two books in the botanical field, which Corder had illustrated. There was also a letter from Connie Voss which started "Dear Nature Boy. . . ." Louis Voss was an anthropologist at Holtz Academy in Boston where Corder also lectured occasionally on the art of scientific illustration. A month ago he had started a sabbatical year, which he was spending in Europe—first with a quiet winter in England, where he hoped to paint and pursue his favorite hobby, which was shooting, and later working over his biography of John James Audubon.

Then in the spring he was going to hire a camper and tour the rest of Europe, with special attention to the routes followed by Audubon in his European Journals.

Connie didn't have much news to give him, just gossip about the department and about the five Voss children. As he put the letter away in his wallet, the waiter came down the car with a napkin on his arm like a stage butler, and announced that tea was being served in the restaurant car.

Mrs. Fleming had told him about the tea. It passed the journey, she had said in her cool voice.

He had seen the advertisement in a newspaper which he had picked up in a bar in Chelsea where he'd been waiting for Richey Morgan. Richey Morgan was an old friend of his and was now a tennis coach at a London indoor club, and Corder was staying with him until he'd fixed up a pad of his own. For two or three days he'd been combing the estate departments of several big stores trying to find a quiet country place that he could rent for the winter. But all they could offer him were Georgian manor houses, mostly in Ireland, and a couple of castles in Scotland.

In the property column of the London *Evening News* the advertisement said: "Country cottage to let for the winter, somewhat isolated in delightful Constable country. Two beds, garage if required." It was the word "somewhat" that had charmed him, and if it was really isolated there might be some rough shooting with no one to bother him. Then and there he had pushed his way through the pale faces and dark suits to the phone booth in the corner. Mrs. Fleming sounded remote, and her voice was faintly staccato, like a voice from an old movie.

"No, it isn't rented yet. Are you living on the base?"

"The base?"

"There's an American Air Force base at Woodbridge. They often rent houses in the district. I thought. . . ."

"I'm staying in London," Corder said. "But I want somewhere for the winter."

"It's extremely lonely. I don't know whether my husband made that clear in the advertisement."

"He did say it was . . . somewhat isolated."

"Have you any family?" And after a moment's hesitation she added, "The cottage isn't really suitable for children, you see. There's a pond that's quite deep. . . ."

"No, I don't have any family, Mrs. Fleming."

"I see. Who is it speaking?"

"My name is Corder." Then he waited patiently while she detailed all the things that were wrong with the place and why it wouldn't suit him in particular.

"There's electricity, of course, but only bottled gas for

cooking, and the drainage is by septic tank. It's rather far from the village but there is a shop there. I'm afraid they're a bit hopeless. They don't deliver."

He waited while she told him about other things. A laundry truck came once a week; there was no washing machine. And the garage was used for storage so there was really only room for a very small car.

Did he have a car? No, he was hoping to get a car when he settled in.

"Well. . . ."

Corder was already used to British methods of trading. It wasn't so much a soft sell as a nonsell. They set out to convince you there was nothing doing, that what you wanted wasn't good for you, and finally that they didn't want you to have it. And it worked every time, because in the end you bought it out of sheer cussedness and frustration.

He said, "Look, Mrs. Fleming. . . . None of these things you mention bother me at all. I'm a painter and I just want somewhere quiet to work. And in between times I'd like to do a little shooting if there's some around."

"It's mostly farming country. You'd have to get permission."

"Well, I can go into that."

There was a long silence and from somewhere in the room behind her he heard a clock start chiming slowly.

"You do realize there's no central heating?" There was almost triumph in her voice. "Just oil stoves. . . . And an electric heater in the bedroom."

"That will do fine. Look, Mrs. Fleming," he said firmly, "I'd like to come down tomorrow to see it and if it's suitable I'd like to move in before the weekend. If you could give me the address. . . ."

He wrote it down carefully on the edge of the news-paper. Burdock Cottage, Easton, Nr. Woodbridge, Suffolk.

She followed it up with another British custom—that of explaining in great detail how to get from A to B. He got off at Woodbridge Station, and the village was about twelve miles inland, the crisp voice went on and on while he doodled. It was then she told him about having tea on the train.

"Well, thank you very much, Mrs. Fleming. I'm sure I'll be able to find my way all right. And I'll look forward to meeting you tomorrow." As he made his way back to the bar he realized that another good old British custom had been observed. Nobody had mentioned money.

The train was running through flat country which was cool and green in the autumn light. The late corn had been cut and twice he saw pheasants running for cover through the stubble. He felt the same atavistic thrill he always got.

It was curious that Louis and Connie Voss didn't un-derstand about shooting. They were always lecturing him about it in terrible Freudian clichés, telling him how sub-consciously he was worried about his virility and that his gun was only a phallic symbol. If he couldn't get birds with one, he had to get a different kind of bird with the other. The whole thing was compensatory. Corder had to admit he found them both a bit intense at times.

The compartment emptied out at Ipswich and he was able to put his feet up on the seat. After fifteen minutes he saw sunlight on an estuary and a fretwork of yacht masts. Only two other people got off at the station, which had a sign saying "This is an unmanned Halt." He crossed a yard where no cabs waited and started up a street to where he could see a church tower. It was a pleasant market town with mellow gable roofs and not much traffic. It didn't look as if anything violent could happen here.

It would never be High Noon in Church Street, Woodbridge.

After Rosemary had brought the tea tray sometime about eleven, Denis Fleming telephoned the Enquiry Office at Ipswich Station. The girl there assured him that the London train had been on time and had only just left. Denis sipped his tea. There were only two trains from London in the morning and he had already checked on the earlier one. Mr. Corder couldn't have been on it, or Louise would have telephoned him by now. He waited the fifteen minutes impatiently, then he bent to a drawer of his desk and took out his Ross binoculars again. They were wrapped in an antistatic cloth. He carried them to the window and standing back to the left-hand side he pushed his glasses onto the top of his head and looked down past the Guild Hall to the entrance of Church Street. There was no taxi stand at the station, so unless Mr. Corder picked one up by chance he would have to walk up to the square. It was a Wednesday and only a handful of people moved on the pavement.

Denis rested the eyepiece against his moustache, pushing gently at the bristle. Perhaps Mr. Corder wouldn't come after all, perhaps he had seen another advertisement, one for a cottage more suitable. It was unlikely that he would bother to call Louise and tell her. Then he saw a tall man come out of Church Street and start crossing toward the Guild Hall.

He was walking unhurriedly, with a long stride, and he wore a turtleneck sweater under his tweed suit. Although his hair at the temples was tipped with gray Denis thought he looked about thirty-five, but the most notice-able thing about him was his large, sloping shoulders, as if he might have been some kind of athlete.

Denis centered the glasses on Mr. Corder's face, that is if it *was* Mr. Corder. It was a strong face with a wide mouth, and looking at it Denis tried to read the character within. For although it was important that Mr. Corder should be physically personable, his morals were of even greater importance.

He lowered the glasses as the taxi moved off across the Square and disappeared up Theatre Street. In less than an hour he would be certain whether it had been Mr. Corder or not.

Louise had promised to telephone the moment he arrived.

[2]

Corder had seen a cab parked in front of the Guild Hall and he was halfway through telling the driver the address when the driver said: "Oh, you mean the Fleming place."

"That's right."

And as they drove out of the square the driver said, "Are you from the base?"

Corder said no, he wasn't. He sat back, closing his eyes, and after a moment he heard the driver push a button on the radio. They followed the bypass for a mile or two, then took off through narrow country lanes. The sky shook once as a flight of jets went over, heading toward the coast.

He saw EASTON printed on a sign and they went through a village and out the other side. When they came to some tumbledown park gates the driver turned in. The driveway wound around through a stand of chestnuts and then went down into a dip. There was a cottage there with a steep-pitched roof and oak-mullioned windows. As they drew level, Corder saw the pond. Then they were climbing up a rise to where a larger house was standing behind a screen of buddleia and Italian poplars. The cab stopped on a paved forecourt and Corder got out in the shadow of an Elizabethan house with a lot of brick trim and curly chimney stacks. He paid off the driver and went into the porch and pulled an iron bell handle. An old rocker bell clanged away deep in the house and a distant door slammed. He waited for some time, and he was wondering whether to ring again when the door opened quietly and suddenly.

Mrs. Fleming said, "Yes? What is it?"

"My name is Corder. I called about the cottage."

"Yes, of course. Won't you come in." She closed the door behind him and then went past him with a skip. "Will you wait here, Mr. Corder. I won't keep you a moment." The room was comfortable and chintzy and there was a lavender walk beyond the french window. He stood looking out and in the distance he heard the tinkle of a phone.

Mrs. Fleming was about his own age, with a dark and watchful manner which wasn't unattractive. Corder thought she was a bit schoolmistressy, with her glasses and pleated skirt.

In the dining room Louise waited for her husband to answer. The phone had been picked up by Rosemary in the showroom and the extension button was clicking steadily.

At last Denis said, "Fleming here."

"I thought I'd let you know he's arrived."

"I thought I saw him in the square. Did he come in a taxi?"

"Yes."

"Then it was probably him."

There was silence for a moment. Louise waited, frowning. Then Denis said drily, "Do you think he's agreeable?"

"Well, he looks all right. Time will tell how agreeable he is."

"Quite."

"Do you think you should meet him. . . . I mean there's the money side, I'm not very good at that."

"Just tell him it's fifty pounds a month, payable in advance, and he pays his own fuel bills. If he seems really put off, then say for three months or more it would only be forty. It's still very reasonable."

"All right."

"Don't forget to turn on the electricity."

There was a click as Denis hung up. Louise waited a moment, smoothing her hair nervously.

When she came back Corder was standing by the french window.

"It's a fine place you have here, Mrs. Fleming. It must be pretty old."

"About five hundred years."

"Really," said Corder. When he turned around she was standing awkwardly in the center of the room. "Just before Columbus."

"Yes." Her hands came together, then parted again.

He said, "I noticed an empty cottage when we were driving in. Was that the one?"

"Yes. Yes it was. Shall we go down there now? We can go out that way." She waited while he opened the french window and when he glanced back she hadn't moved. She said, "Do go on."

He walked out onto the brick terrace between the lavender bushes and after a moment she came out and moved parallel with him toward the stone steps. They followed a walk through thickets of shrubbery. Louise Fleming said, "It's a picture in the spring when the forsythia's out," and when Corder stopped to look back at the house she added hurriedly, "I should make it clear that the cottage is quite on its own. You have your own entrance onto the road. And the trees screen you completely from our house."

They crossed the main driveway and went on across rough ground. There was a ditch halfway to the cottage lined with crack willows, and after he'd jumped it he turned to offer her a hand. But she was already crossing further down. A moorhen went skittering away into the trees.

When he joined her again she said, "The ditch drains into the pond, actually."

They came up to the back of the cottage and she bent and took a key from under a doormat. There was an empty milk bottle standing beside a garbage can.

"The milk is left by your postbox up on the lane."

Corder followed her carefully through a tangle of blackberry around to the front door. She opened it and went into a pleasant room that was chintzy as well, and with a high-beamed ceiling. The fireplace was nearly the width of the room.

"This is great," Corder said. "Just what I was looking for."

"Nobody has lived in it since my parents were here a year ago. Well . . . not *really* lived in it. We did try someone but it wasn't a success." She came back from opening a window and ran her finger lightly across the round table, looking for dust. "It's bigger than it looks."

A staircase rose centrally with heavy oak newel-posts. Corder followed her up onto the landing. "That's the main bedroom," she said and pushed open the door.

He went in and looked around the square room. There was a double bed with folded blankets, a mahogany chest of drawers, and a wardrobe. A faded reproduction of "The Light of the World" was hanging crookedly over the fireplace and over the bed was a porcelain plaque which said "Bless This House."

From the landing Mrs. Fleming said, "I'm afraid we don't supply linen. You'd have to bring that yourself."

"I've got my own."

When he went out, she'd opened the other doors on the landing and was waiting stiffly against the stair rail. He looked into another, smaller bedroom and then the bathroom. Mrs. Fleming coughed. She said, "The water is also heated by gas. There's a multipoint heater." She heard the sudden clank as he pulled the chain when he came out, smiling at her.

"Works okay."

She looked faintly startled before turning away and going downstairs again. He followed her through a short passage to the kitchen. There were gingham curtains at the window, and the kitchen table, the stove, and the sink were old-fashioned but clean.

"Mrs. Abbott was here two days ago. She comes to

clean for me once a week. If you need any help I'm sure she. . . ."

"I prefer to look after myself. I'm pretty domesticated."

She opened a door in the corner to show a steep flight of steps.

"There's a cellar down there. . . . It's quite large. The gas drums are stored there. Go down if you wish."

"No, I'm sure that's all in order."

She closed the door and they went back to the living room.

She sat down, smoothing the front of her pleated skirt.

"Do you think it will be suitable?"

"I do. I like it very much."

"I'm so glad." There was silence in the room. From somewhere beyond the open front door came the soft, contented call of a wood pigeon.

It was too idyllic to last and Corder felt brutal when he said, "How much is the rent?"

"Didn't it say in the advertisement?"

"No."

"Oh dear." She hesitated. "I thought . . . that is, my husband thought that fifty pounds a month would be reasonable. You'd pay for your electricity and gas, of course." After another pause she added, "And of course we'd expect you to replace any breakages."

"Well, that suits me, Mrs. Fleming." He went over to the round table and sat down. While he was writing a check for a hundred and thirty-one dollars he said, "I'd very much like to inquire into the possibilities of shooting."

"Well, since you mentioned it on the phone, I've spoken to Mr. McDougall who owns the farm next door.

These woods are all his and he's quite happy for you to shoot anytime, provided you are on your own."

"I understand."

"He said it's not a good year for birds because we had a wet June, but there are plenty of hares. And pigeons, of course. I said you'd call. He's a mile further on."

"Thanks very much." He carried the check across and she took it as if almost by accident and folded it immediately in two.

"Thank you. When do you intend to move in?"

"I thought in a couple of days. Before the weekend."

Louise Fleming stood up and moved away. "Well, that's settled," she said and smiled at him. "I'm so glad."

At the door she said, "If you find there's anything you need which we haven't supplied, or if you have any problems, don't hesitate to speak to me or my husband."

There was honeysuckle around the door, still heavy with yellow blossom. He walked down the path looking at a neat bed of roses while she fiddled with the key. "You may as well have it now," she said. She joined him and he pocketed the key. "I'm sorry I can't run you back to the station . . . I'm expecting a friend. Would you like me to call you a taxi from the house?"

"If you don't mind, I'd like to walk around, get the lay of the land. I'll make for the village. I can always call one up from there."

She was facing him and suddenly she thrust out a hand between them. "It's been so nice meeting you." When he took her hand, which was soft and dry, she momentarily gripped his own like a man. "Goodbye, Mr. Corder."

"Goodbye . . . and thanks."

She stood in the rose garden watching him move away

and follow a path that ran parallel to the driveway. She noticed how immense his shoulders seemed. He must be very powerful, she decided.

Corder walked slowly through thickets of bramble. And when he got near the road a flock of rooks flew out of the chestnut trees, and climbed raucously above him. There was a wicket gate onto the lane with a mailbox fixed onto one of the posts. He turned east toward the village, feeling the sun warm on his back.

Louise Fleming could hear the phone ringing while she was still on the lower driveway. She didn't quicken her steps because she knew he wouldn't hang up, that he would stay at the other end transfixed by his anxiety. She went up the flagged steps lazily flicking a switch of crack willow and walked across the french window. When she reached the telephone, she took it off the hook and held it for a moment at arm's length.

A dwarf's voice said, "Hello? Louise? Are you there?" She raised it at last, watching herself in the mirror as she always did. "Yes, I'm here."

"Has he gone? Is everything all right?"

"Everything's fine. He gave me a check for a month in advance. He liked the cottage very much."

"But what did you think of *him?*"

"Oh, you needn't worry. He's human." And after a pause she added, "In fact he's very human."

"When's he moving in?"

"On Friday."

"He isn't wasting any time. You can tell me all about it tonight. I have to go now, I'm doing an estimate over at Waldringfield."

"Goodbye, darling."

After she'd hung up she stood there for a moment flicking at the telephone with the willow switch, bringing it down quite hard as if the phone were a living thing. An extension almost of his personality. And she was inflicting a punishment.

Corder followed the lane toward the village and passed the main entrance again. The Fleming house wasn't visible through the hedge of poplars and buddleia, and he went striding on to where he could see a square Norman church tower. The flag of St. George drooped from the flagstaff on top of it. He walked down the village street where only a few late roses bloomed in the gardens of a neat row of cottages. The church clock was striking midday as he went into the cool, dark bower of The White Hart.

A woman was singing in a kitchen somewhere at the back. Corder crossed a floor of quarry tiles and waited. After a moment he saw a small silver bell on the bar. He shook it loudly. The singing stopped and a girl came into the bar, walking slowly in slippers that dragged. She was very thin, with an open face, like a freckled orchid.

She waited, watching him across the polished mahogany counter, until Corder said, "A beer, please . . . a small one."

"Mild or bitter?"

"Bitter."

She turned away and bent to draw it. Although she was young there was already a cluster of veins showing high up on her calf. Maybe there were half a dozen kids in the back, Corder thought, or maybe she carried the barrels in herself. She put the beer down and took his money;

then she came to stand opposite him again.

"If you're busy don't worry about me," Corder said pleasantly.

"I'm not busy." Her voice had the faint singsong of the district. "Are you from the base?"

"No." Before he'd really thought about telling her, Corder heard himself saying, "As a matter of fact I've just rented a cottage up the road."

"Oh yes."

"Burdock cottage."

She was about to speak when the church clock started dinning out midday. Somewhere on the shelves two glasses set up a shivering echo. Corder waited when the last note died away, but she didn't go on.

He said, "So I'll be seeing you again."

"Won't your wife find it lonely?"

"I'm not married." He smiled. "And if I find it lonely I can always walk down here."

She didn't smile back. Instead she took a cloth and began to wipe the counter rhythmically. She said, "The last one came sometimes. Mostly at weekends."

"Who?"

"The man who was there before. He only left a month ago."

Corder remembered Mrs. Fleming saying that they had tried someone but he hadn't *really* lived in it, whatever that meant. He said, "He didn't like it, apparently. . . ."

"Oh, he loved it. He was there nearly a year."

"What happened? Why did he leave?"

"Nobody knows. He just vanished. One day he was there, the next he was gone. They say he owed a month's rent."

Corder finished his tankard and put it down. "Well, I

won't do that." As she took his glass he asked her about getting a cab.

"There's one at the garage a little way on. If it's out they'll telephone Woodbridge for you."

"Thanks very much."

Corder had his hand on the latch when she said hurriedly, "Funny thing is you look just like him. When I came into the bar and you were standing against the light I thought it was him come back again. He was just your build . . . enormous shoulders he had."

[3]

Denis Fleming drove around the house and as he approached the barn doors he activated the electronic switch with his headlights and they rose smoothly into the roof space. He parked neatly beside Louise's Renault. Walking to the side door his hand stroked the hood of the Renault with a gesture that had become habitual. It was still warm. Then he remembered that it was Wednesday, the day she did her duty with the old people at the almshouse in Framlingham. He flicked a switch to close the main doors and went out by a side door onto the drive. The sky to the west was full of bloody violence—the way it always was in Suffolk where the London haze refracted the last of the sun into a blaze rather like a Michelangelo illustration for the Inferno. Denis crunched around the house thinking of the barbecue spit in his window. He had an analytic rather than a poetic mind. He went into the hall and hung up his hat and jacket and put on the sagging cardigan he always kept there. It had been patched with leather at the elbows and cuffs.

He went through to the kitchen. Louise said, "Hello, darling," as she heard the door close. Then she came down to kiss his cheek lightly. "I'm nearly done, just putting the rice on."

As she walked back to the stove he looked after her, blinking.

"Well, go on," he said hurriedly. "Tell me what happened. . . ."

"I'll tell you while we nave our drink." She turned around. "I think I'll have a sherry tonight." And when he still hadn't moved she said, "Go on, darling. Get it all cozy."

He crossed the hall again and went into the living room. When he turned on the electric heater the log simulator set up another pattern of hellfire. He got glasses from the corner cupboard and poured a whisky for himself and Louise's very dry sherry. As he waited by the window, watching the lurid sky again, he heard her come in and pick up her glass, and then the familiar creaking sigh of the chaise as she sat down and put her feet up.

He said, "What did you wear?"

"That old pleated skirt and a paisley blouse. I must have looked really dreadful."

"How old do you think he is?"

"Oh, somewhere in his late thirties, *I* thought. He's quite good-looking."

Denis went to sit in a wing chair opposite her, and drew up a tripod table for his glass.

Louise said, "He looked more English than American. Except that his voice is American, of course. He was wearing a nice Harris tweed suit."

"Did he say much about himself?"

"Not really. He has a private income, I should imagine. He said he just wanted to paint and shoot." Louise drained her glass and held it out to him. He carried it to the sideboard and refilled it.

"Well, he's come to the right place." Denis gave her back her glass. "Did he mention his family at all?"

"No. He didn't mention anyone else."

Later they ate at the table in the kitchen, and afterward while she stacked the dishes in the dishwasher and tidied up, Denis went into the dining room where his roll-top desk was. Corder's check was on the top, drawn on the Chase Manhattan Bank. Denis opened up the desk and sat down. He heard Louise go back to the sitting room and turn on the television and afterward the intermittent surging laughter of a comedy program. Denis opened a small marble-backed ledger and headed a new page "Cottage Accounts." On the left-hand side he wrote, "To Rent Received £50.00." Then he opened his document case and put the check away. He put the ledger back in the drawer and sat there quietly staring at his spread hands.

He often sat alone in this way with his weight slightly on his hands as if he were at the console of an organ about to play some deeply considered voluntary. He'd been seated like this when they'd brought Louise back from the nursing home after her third miscarriage.

Philip Gander, the surgeon, had driven her back himself and in the hall she'd said noisily, "Sorry, darling, but that's another one down the drain."

He'd stood there blinking, helpless. "Never mind, darling. As long as you're all right, that's the main thing."

"Oh, I'm fine." It wasn't until she collapsed against him that he realized how drunk she was. "And I've still got *you*, darling. That's the main thing too."

Philip Gander had moved discreetly into the living room and Denis could hear his lighter clicking. Louise said loudly, "They want me to rest rather a lot, so I'm going to start right now." And at the foot of the stairs she'd thrown off his arm. "I don't need any help, darling. What I want is for you and Philip to bring me up a large gin in five minutes and we'll have a coming-home party in the bedroom."

"Are you sure. . . ."

"Sure I'm sure." And she had weaved away gracefully up the stairs.

Philip Gander was standing in front of the fire when he went in, looking watchful. Denis closed the door before he said, "She's pissed."

"Doctor's orders. I've filled her up on the way home."

"I suppose you know what you're doing."

"I hope so. A woman has a sense of failure after a miscarriage. She feels she's let the partnership down. This is the third time and her sense of failure is cumulative, so you must be particularly careful how you go."

"I'll look after her. I can let the business freewheel for a few days."

"That's what you mustn't do. For God's sake don't be sympathetic or she'll go to pieces. Just be the same as usual."

40

When Denis picked up the thistle decanter Philip Gander shook his head. "No thanks, I've had enough." Then he said, "Another pregnancy could be dangerous. Do you know what I mean?"

"You want to take out her works."

"Christ, no . . . not a hysterectomy. Just tie up a tube or two, that's all. It won't spoil the fun for either of you."

Denis was so long looking into his drink that Philip Gander said carelessly, "Of course you can ask for another opinion."

Denis swallowed half of his whisky, then dabbed at his bristle moustache with a handkerchief before he said primly, "No. No, I'm quite satisfied if that's what you recommend." He'd never quite realized it could come to this, he thought that nowadays there were drugs, there were other ways. . . . He thought of the crib under the stairs and the box of worn-out toys her mother had sent. He thought of Fleming & Son Limited. . . .

"When . . . when shall I tell her?" In spite of himself his voice fractured slightly.

"Oh, you don't need to worry about that. I told her over the second gin."

"I see."

Philip Gander threw his cigarette carelessly into the garden and came down the room. "I've got to get back . . . I'm on call in the emergency ward from two o'clock."

"You've been very kind. . . ."

"Come out to the car with me. I've got some tablets for her. You'd better look after them. . . ."

It wasn't till a week after this that he'd brought home the boxer pup. He'd picked it up from the kennel in the morning with a woven dog basket lined with gingham, and he'd taken it out to the house just before lunch. He opened the front door very quietly and popped them both inside and waited just long enough to hear her surprised voice. Then he'd gone back to the car.

She didn't phone during the afternoon as he'd half-expected and when he got back in the evening she'd kissed him as usual. Over her shoulder he saw the basket already set tidily beside the fireplace with the puppy asleep in it.

Then she'd whispered, "Doggy's dead," and slapped his face.

He'd waited frozen for a long time, afraid of what a word or even the twitch of a muscle might do. But nothing happened. He never knew how it had died, whether she had suffocated it or strangled it. It was just dead.

Later when he carried it out of the house she called after him quite calmly, "Bury it in the rose bed. The blood is supposed to be very good for them. Perhaps that's why they have such marvelous roses at the nursing home."

And later still when they had gone to bed she held him very tightly. "Poor Denis," she whispered, "you do *try,* don't you?"

He said, "We'll work something out."

Well, they certainly had worked something out, he thought wryly. He'd kept running into the woman from the kennel who always asked about the puppy until eventually he told her it had been put away. She'd offered a replacement and he'd had great difficulty in stopping her delivering one to the house.

From the living room a news announcer had started to speak in a voice that was relevant and serious, and a minute later Denis heard a click as the television was switched off. He reached up quickly to turn on the desk lamp. When Louise tapped on the door and looked in, the ledger was open in front of him again.

42

"The television is so boring tonight I'm going to go up and read in bed." She walked idly around the dining table and straightened a mat. "Are you going to be late?"

"Another half hour. I'll probably have a nightcap."

"Yes, have a nightcap. It will help you relax." He heard the door close.

Speaking to himself he said, "But I am relaxed." Then he noticed that his fists were clenched.

The master bedroom was above the dining room so that as he sat there he could hear her crossing to and fro as she undressed. Then the door to the hall opened as she went along to the bathroom to brush her teeth. Denis put the ledger away and waited till she came back. When he heard the bedsprings creak he stood up at last and picked up his case. He went quietly across the hall into the still-warm living room. The curtains were drawn except for the floor-deep ones across the french window, and he drew these before moving to the mantelpiece.

He felt behind the clock for a moment until he found the screwdriver he kept there. Then he went to the record player in the corner and moved it sideways a couple of inches. He removed the four screws from the perforated panel on the back and lifted it away. The tape recorder was built neatly into the rear of the cabinet with a vertical deck using special-duty long-run tape. Denis opened his case and took out a fresh tape and switched it with the empty spool, which he then switched with the old tape. He threaded it, ran off a little, then checked the time switch at the side. It was set to start at noon precisely. He replaced the panel and lifted the player back into the corner, taking care the legs fitted the same dents in the carpet. He put the tape away in his case and closed it; then he put the screwdriver back behind the clock.

He set his case down in the hall, walked around the house as he always did before going up, checking that the doors were locked and all the lights were off. When he went into the bedroom Louise was still awake but her book was laid aside. He undressed inside the walk-in closet, hanging up his clothes as he took them off. Her light was out when he went back.

As he slid between the covers she murmured, "What have you been doing?"

"Just a few accounts. We'll have to keep track of what we spend on the cottage."

"Oh, God . . . does that mean we have to pay tax on the rent?"

"I'm afraid so."

"Why do they have to tax everything," she said drowsily.

After a small silence Denis said, "How much was the advertisement, by the way?"

"Just under £20, I think . . . or just over. We had to run it three times. In fact Mr. Corder was the twenty-third person to answer." She turned over in the bed, settling for sleep. "It takes all the profit, really."

From somewhere in the woods behind the house came the throbbing call of a tawny owl. Denis switched off his own bedside light.

Then he said carefully, into the darkness, "It's always worthwhile spending money on advertising . . . if it helps you to get exactly what you want."

Corder spent Thursday packing up. In the morning he called the Grosvenor Street branch of the Chase Manhattan Bank and gave them his new address and asked them to arrange credit for him with a local bank in Woodbridge. Then he caught a bus to Sloane Square and bought two sets of striped bedsheets and pillowcases to match. Thursday evening he spent drinking with Richey.

In the morning Richey called the Sports Club to tell them he wouldn't be in until late and insisted on taking Corder to the station at Liverpool Street. Richey drove an upright, antique Rolls-Royce with yellow wheels, which made a great impression on passersby.

Together they carried his gun case and easel and the rest of the baggage downstairs and stowed it in the car. As they drove regally along the Thames embankment Richey said, "I don't know how you'll stick it."

"I've spent the winter in quieter places, Richey."

"Man can't live by bread alone," Richey said. "You'll be welcome any weekend." And when Corder didn't answer, he said, "Or I could bring Brenda and Smarty down and stay with you."

"I'd rather you didn't."

They drove down a ramp where taxicabs were parked and a porter unloaded the car.

Corder and Richey shook hands with mockery.

Richey said, "Best of luck, old man," as if he was bound on a hazardous mission.

"See you in the spring." He watched Richey climb back into the Rolls and sweep smoothly away into the traffic stream before he turned and followed the porter.

The train left Ipswich and he was alone with a thin, attractive Englishwoman. Her gray eyes examined Corder, Corder's baggage, and the landscape beyond the windows, all with the same indiscriminate vagueness. She had a wide mouth with faint cat lines at each end which deepened now and then in response to some inner thought. When

they arrived at Woodbridge she left the compartment
ahead of him. Corder stacked his baggage on the platform
and watched the train pull away.

Then he put his document case under his arm and
set off for the Market Square. As he came out of the station
an MGB with the top down was parked across the ramp.

"Can I give you a lift? For some odd reason there's
never a taxi here." She was wearing sunglasses and a head-
scarf but he recognized the sculptured lips.

"Thanks very much." He walked around and stepped
into the other seat.

"Are you on holiday?"

"Well, not really. I'm staying for quite a while. I've
rented a cottage at a place called Easton."

"Easton," she said. Then after a pause, "Does it
belong to a friend of mine called Archie Forbes?"

"No. This one belongs to someone called Fleming."

"Oh, I see."

She started the car at last and drove slowly out of the
yard and up to the first set of lights. Waiting there, she
said, "My name's Stella Ferris. My husband and I live at
Wickham Market, which isn't far away. Shall I drop you in
the square? There's usually a taxi there."

"Anywhere will do. . . . I'm going to need a car
myself so I thought I'd find a dealer. . . ."

"I know just the place on the Melton Road." As they
weaved through the narrow streets she said, "Are your
family joining you?"

"I'm not married."

"Oh." They came to more lights. "Then what on
earth are you going to do at Easton?"

"Well, I'm hoping to revise this book and do some

painting. . . ." Corder twisted in his seat, hesitating. It always sounded so bloody pretentious.

"I'm sorry, I didn't hear you."

"I'm revising this book on Audubon . . . and I hope to be painting some wildlife myself. . . ."

"How fascinating. I noticed your gun case in the carriage. My husband, Colonel Ferris, has several hundred acres of shooting. I'll see if. . . ."

"Organized shooting isn't really my scene, Mrs. Ferris. . . . I'd rather. . . ."

"Oh, don't worry. We're frightfully disorganized." And with an air of finality she said, "I'll speak to my husband."

"Well. . . ."

But they were sweeping onto the forecourt of the service station. Stella Ferris didn't stop the engine. The sunglasses watched him blindly as he climbed out. The cat lines deepened into a brief smile. "Goodbye."

Corder waved vaguely.

As he walked in the direction of a row of cars, a man with well-slicked hair and a regimental tie came out of the sales office. A moment later he was explaining to Corder that there wasn't much in at the moment and he doubted whether they could really be of help.

Corder waited patiently for the nonsell to end.

[4]

He got lost once on his way out to the cottage but he found the village in the end and stopped there to load up with groceries.

He parked alongside the cottage and unloaded. Afterward he went up and opened the garage door, but it was so full of junk there wasn't enough room for the Land-Rover. He poked around for a while. There was a workbench under the window and beyond it a dusty piano. He raised the lid and struck a note idly. Then he moved on past a litter of steamer trunks, apple boxes, some Victorian chairs with the stuffing pulled out, to a rusty bicycle. He went back to the cottage.

The studio easel was set up in the middle of the sitting room and the windows were open on a bright sky with only a few cirrus clouds.

There was silence except for the chattering of sparrows fighting in an ivy-covered beech. It came in long bursts, like the fire of diminutive machine guns. Corder felt as at home as he could ever be. As anyone in a rented place could ever be.

He said "Coffee" to himself out loud and went into the kitchen to unpack the groceries. There was no coffee-pot, only a teapot. It was while he was hunting for the coffeepot that he found the note under the saltcellar on the sideboard. It was signed Louise Fleming, and written in rather thick Gothic letters. It said, "Dear Mr. Corder— I've asked the tradesmen to call when they're passing. A butcher calls on Tuesday and the baker daily, except Saturdays, at about 11. Do let me know if there is anything we have forgotten to supply. With best wishes, Louise Fleming."

He crumpled it up and threw it away. He wouldn't trouble her for a coffeepot. He'd make do with a saucepan.

Denis said, "A Land-Rover."

"Yes, rather an ancient one. He's parked it by the cottage."

"I hope it won't cut up the drive."

In the short ensuing silence Denis knew that she wanted him to suggest that she should go down and see if Corder was settling in; she did not want to suggest it herself, she did not want to appear to be rushing things.

He said, "I thought of coming back early today. Aren't we having dinner with Eliot?"

"Yes."

"Well, if I come back early I can stop at the cottage and see if everything is all right."

Louise said, "I do think one of us should check."

Denis looked at his watch. "I should be through in about an hour. Home at about five."

"Don't say. . . ."

While she was hesitating, Denis said, "Don't worry. I know what not to say." He hung up and leaned back in his chair. He hadn't meant to suggest going there. Words had somehow rushed out while he was still thinking about it. On the whole he really would have preferred Louise to go down and for himself to remain uninvolved with Corder at present. He leaned forward over the folder of factory invoices but his concentration had gone. Instead he found himself wondering what sort of painter Corder was. Did he have a lot of glamorous models around, for instance? Because that wouldn't do at all. He closed the folder on his desk and stood up to carry it to the filing cabinet.

Then he changed his jacket and opened the document case on his desk. He took out the tape that was there and locked it in a drawer from which he took a fresh tape. Then he went down to the workshop.

Only Barney and one of the men were working there.

"I'm going home early," he told Barney. "Will you lock up?"

"Sure, Mr. Fleming. Peter wants to know if he can go up to London next Thursday. He'll make the time up."

"If it suits you."

"Well, we're not inundated."

"All right. Good night, Barney."

He went on through the showroom. "I'm off, Rosemary. See you tomorrow."

51

"Bye, Mr. Fleming."

When he'd left the town behind he didn't speed up but drove slowly in the left-hand lane, thinking about what he'd say to Corder. He wasn't good at casual relationships, which was why Louise arranged their social life. As he drove through the village he was conscious of his heart beating more quickly than usual. He couldn't decide whether to drive up to the house first and walk down or whether to stop on the way. It would be more natural to stop on the way. He slowed at the entrance of the drive as a hen pheasant ran stupidly in front of the car.

When the cottage came into view the Land-Rover had gone. He had just let his breath go with relief when he saw it, parked in the lee of the garage. He slowed down and stopped. For a moment he sat there aimlessly watching the cottage, then he started the engine again. Suddenly he seemed to be in an angry panic. I can't drive on now, he thought, and instead he drove the car slightly off the drive and parked it. He got out and, slamming the door loudly, went through the wicket gate into the rose garden Only the white roses, Iceberg, were still in bloom. He walked more slowly up the path, hoping that perhaps Corder would have heard the car door and come out. But the cottage remained silent.

Perhaps he's gone for a walk, Denis thought, and felt again a quick wave of relief. He raised the dolphin knocker and gave it a quick rat-a-tat. The silence went on and he was just turning away when the bedroom window opened.

Corder called, "Go right in. It's not locked. I'll be down in a minute."

"Oh, thank you very much." Denis was annoyed that his voice sounded faintly shallow and unsteady. The window was slammed shut before he finished.

He raised the lever of the latch and pushed open the door. There was a fishing rod standing in the umbrella stand. Denis closed the door and moved uneasily to the center of the room. There were huge folders on the table and a jam jar full of grasses and wild flowers. The gun case was leaning against it. Then he saw the easel with a drawing pad on it. Across the open page of the drawing pad Corder had written in large capitals, "Man goeth forth to his work." Denis didn't smile when he read it.

Then Corder's voice called from the bedroom, "Shan't be long."

Denis went nearer to the foot of the stairs. He said loudly, "It's nothing important. . . . I'll call back later." He waited but there was no reply, only the faint thud of Corder moving around. A door slammed and Denis shied away suddenly and stood by the window. Corder came down the stairs two at a time and swung on the newel-post. "Hello there. What can I do for you?" He moved across to stand by the fireplace as if he'd always belonged there. He was wearing a sweater and washed-out jeans that were ragged around the pockets.

"I . . . I thought I'd better introduce myself. My name's Fleming."

"Fleming? Oh, *Fleming*. How do you do, sir." He came forward and they shook hands awkwardly. Denis wished he hadn't said "sir."

Denis said, "Well, you . . . you seem to be settled in. I really called to see if there was anything I could do for you."

"No, I seem to have everything, thank you, sir. And I should like to say I like the place very much. I think it's most attractive. If you knew how peaceful it is after London. . . ."

53

"Yes, it is pretty. We did it up for my mother, actually, but she only likes to come for a week or two in the summer and it seems a pity to leave it empty. My wife said you were interested in doing a bit of shooting. You won't shoot too close to the house, I hope?"

"No, of course not, sir." Corder gestured with one of his biggish hands. "Won't you sit down? If it's not too early I can offer you a whisky. . . ."

"No, thank you. I . . . I haven't got long. I was going to say if you wanted organized shooting that's more difficult."

"No, I'm quite happy to shoot around here. Do you shoot yourself, Mr. Fleming?"

"No," Denis said and wished it didn't sound inadequate. "I'm afraid I don't really have time for it nowadays. I've a business in Woodbridge that keeps me pretty busy. I'm an . . . electrical engineer of sorts." Again it sounded in some way inadequate.

"I didn't know that, Mr. Fleming."

With a rush Denis said, "By the way, while I'm here I may as well show you how to change the gas drums. . . . You haven't been down in the cellar yet?"

"No. But I can tell you the hot water system is a lot more efficient than the one I had in London."

Denis hesitated. "Shall I lead the way?"

"Please do," said Corder, waving his big hand again.

They went down the short hallway alongside the staircase. Denis noticed the groceries stacked on the kitchen table and a cup and saucer in the sink. He opened the door to the cellar and switched on the light.

Going carefully down the steps he said, "They're a bit rickety, I'm afraid. We used to store apples here, but it attracted the rats." There were two gray drums standing in the corner, one of them connected to a regulator and a pipe that went up through the ceiling. Denis said, "It was installed when we bought the place. . . . In fact they still had gas lighting. One of these should last you about two or three weeks." He picked up a large wrench from a stone ledge. "When it runs out, all you do is close this valve on top of the drum, then undo the regulator nut." He undid the nut a couple of turns, then tightened it again.

"That shouldn't be too difficult. I've used bottled gas before."

Denis laid the wrench back on the ledge, and dusted his hands. He went toward the steps. "Stinks a bit. That's to let you know if you've got a leak." He started going up again carefully.

Corder walked down to the other end of the cellar before following. There were old cartons stacked in a corner, and in another corner behind a ramp there was a heap of coal dust. A cobweb brushed his face as he turned, and he wiped it away. Fleming was waiting for him at the top of the steps.

Back in the living room Denis took a buff envelope from his pocket and laid it on the circular table. "That's the receipt for the rent you've paid. . . . Just to keep the record straight."

"Thanks."

Corder waited but Denis didn't turn. He was staring at the easel, pressing his moustache lightly with a finger. Then he said suddenly, "Painters always love this part of England. . . . Constable lived not very far from here, and Gainsborough, of course. Are you a portrait painter?"

"No, not really, sir. I'm more interested in natural history. I paint botanical subjects mostly, and butterflies, birds . . . that sort of thing." Corder hoped that Fleming would leave it at that. He hated talking about painting.

Still without turning Denis said, "I've often thought I'd like to have an oil painting of my wife." He laughed uncertainly. "You can call that a commission if ever you feel like doing a portrait."

"Thank you, sir, but I think I'm going to be very much occupied as it is."

Denis moved at last. "I just thought I'd mention it in passing," he said vaguely. He opened the door and stopped again. "Well, then, I'll be getting along. If there's anything you need, don't hesitate to pop up to the house and let us know. In fact just pop up anyway if you feel like it . . . have some coffee . . . my wife's always glad to see anyone. As a matter of fact, it's a bit lonely for her . . . and I'm at work all day, of course."

"That's very kind of you."

"Don't mention it. Well, I'll say cheerio."

"Goodbye, sir. Thank you for calling."

Corder smiled faintly as Denis walked down the path through the rosebushes. It had all been a very British occasion. Maybe he should have brewed tea, he thought guiltily, and offered Fleming a cup. He waved through the window as the car moved off, but Fleming wasn't looking.

Louise Fleming heard the car circle the drive scattering gravel, and stop by the portico. She walked hurriedly through and switched on the electric kettle. A tea tray was laid on the kitchen table with cookies on a plate. Denis always ate two cookies with his tea.

She went back to meet him in the hall, turning her

cheek for him to kiss. "Hello, darling, I've just put the kettle on."

Denis hung up his coat and reached for his cardigan. "What time do we leave?"

"Oh, seven will be early enough. We can have a drink on the way."

He took her arm as she moved toward the kitchen. "I'm looking forward to it." He sat down sideways on one of the wheelback chairs and took a cookie.

Louise looked down at him, one hand on the singing kettle. "Well?"

"What are you going to wear?"

"Oh, that green velvet maxi with my new blouse. Did you call at the cottage?"

He nodded. "It's boiling," he said.

Louise turned away to rinse the pot hurriedly. Then, as she spooned in the tea and poured boiling water, she said, "Well, what happened?"

"You sound quite impatient."

"Don't tease me, darling. What do you think of him?"

Denis smiled at her. He had that faint feeling of euphoria that always followed a period of strain. "I thought he was very nice."

"Is that all?"

"Well, it's always hard to tell with Americans. But he seemed straightforward. He . . . he was making himself comfortable. He'd picked some wild flowers. I think I'll take my tea upstairs while I run the bath. Do you mind if I go first?"

"No, of course not." Louise looked after him curiously as he went to the door.

As if he knew she was watching, he turned and looked

back at her. "I really did like him," he said, "and I told
him to call on you anytime. . . . I thought it would be
better if I suggested it."

Corder walked around the cottage in the dusk with his
Ross binoculars hanging from his neck.

For a long time he stood watching the pond from the
overhang of some crack willows. It was too late to see any
fish that might be there, but after ten minutes he saw a
long chevron of ripples coming across the water almost to
the point where he was standing. Something furry climbed
out onto a stump of ash and he saw it was a water vole.

He held his breath while the small head quested this
way and that. Then it was scratching itself like a dog
before starting to climb one of the ash shoots. Something
must have startled it because it hadn't gone more than a
foot when it plopped back into the water again and swam
away below the surface. Tomorrow he'd bring his sketch-
book, he decided. A moment later he knew what had
startled it as the Flemings' car came sweeping slowly down
the drive. It passed close by the cottage fence and in the
half light he could see Louise Fleming's pale, staring face
turned to the windows. When it disappeared among the
beech and chestnuts he moved on out to the open again
and went around to the back of the house.

Someone had once made an herb bed there. He could
see sage and a clump of pennyroyal. When he came to the
mint, only the seed heads and a few mildewed leaves were
left, and among them he could see something square and
white and luminous. He bent to pick it up, which wasn't
easy. It was a square block of white stone, machine-cut and
with the top scooped out like a bowl.

It was a funeral urn, he realized suddenly, and sure

enough when he turned it around there was an inscription: "Where the weary be at rest. Job III:17." He turned it over again, puzzled, but there was no name and no date, just the quotation.

It was cold in his hand as he walked around the orchard carrying it with him, and when he got back to the house again he held it up briefly to the faint new moon.

"I knew him, Horatio," he murmured. "A fellow of infinite jest."

Then he pitched it back into the herb bed again and went inside.

PART
II

[1]

Corder was awakened by a female mallard quacking loudly and monotonously on the pond.

For two weeks she had awakened him regularly around six o'clock. He rolled out of bed into the chilly air and padded downstairs to put the kettle on the stove. Then he came upstairs again to shave while it boiled. Afterward he got back into bed and drank his coffee there.

Besides the mallard he had also got to know most of his other neighbors. There was the water vole, of course, and there were also fish in the pond. He'd seen them basking on a very hot day. Also, in another corner under some goat willow, a moorhen had built a nest which was as tall and elegant as Elsinore Castle.

Then in one of the walnut trees a little owl had its nest, and it came out every evening to sit on a post near the kitchen window.

Corder finished his coffee and started pulling on corduroy trousers and a heavy sweater. He'd not done much about his human neighbors. He'd called on Mc-Dougall, the farmer up the road, to thank him for being allowed to shoot, and he'd been down to the village pub two or three times for an evening drink. He'd also seen the Flemings occasionally, going to and fro.

Corder went downstairs again in his stocking feet, carrying the coffee mug with him. On the easel was the half-finished pen-and-ink drawing of the vole washing itself. Corder shrugged on his thick shooting coat and dropped half a dozen shells into his side pocket from the carton on the mantelpiece. Then he hooked the side-lock shotgun down from its peg by the door, stepped into his rubber boots, and went out. At the sound of the closing door the mallard took off, climbing away as steeply as a jet. He never shot mallard, because they were poor eating; and besides, he hoped a female might nest nearby when the spring came and hatch her brood there. That would be something to watch.

Corder moved away in the semidarkness to a path he'd trodden out through the woods. It was almost light when he reached the field at the edge of it, and he moved slowly along against the trees, perfectly camouflaged. He had made it a habit to shoot once a day, either at dawn, as now, or in the later afternoon when the birds were coming in to roost, so that the meat larder was already well stocked. During most of the daylight hours he

painted, and around midday he would cook his one big
meal of the day.

Corder was frozen suddenly, watching the ivy cluster
move on an oak tree ahead. He brought the gun halfway
to his shoulder and walked on silently, one pace at a time.
Then he heard the pigeon flapping as it moved around.
He was twenty paces from it when it flew out, suddenly
climbing away to his right front. The gun came cleanly to
his shoulder, automatically deflected ahead, and he fired
almost within a second.

Feathers flew and the bird dropped fifty yards away.
Corder walked out across the newly drilled winter wheat
to pick it up.

Denis Fleming, on the edge of consciousness, heard the
sound of the gunshot echo through the wood.

He opened his eyes in the darkened bedroom and
then gently turned back the covers. Louise was sleeping
deeply and there was light enough for him to see the
glass of water and the bottle of capsules beside her. She
must have awakened during the night and taken a pill,
and it was her habit when this happened to sleep on till
midmorning and let him get his own breakfast. He
showered and dressed and went down to the kitchen. It
was full daylight as he started cracking eggs into the pan,
and he heard the crashing sound of another shot nearer to
the road. He thought of Corder moving silently through
the green morning, the bird rocketing off in fright, and
after the shot its dying fall. He closed his eyes against the
thought. On the way to the car he opened his document
case. The tape was lying in the inner pocket where he'd
placed it last night. He closed the case and put it on the
passenger seat beside him.

His heart was beating a little quicker as he started the engine. He backed the car out, flicking his headlights so that the electronic switch closed the doors automatically. He drove on down past the cottage and slowed before turning out into the lane. It was at that moment he saw Corder walking with his gun on his shoulder and a brace of pigeons dangling limply from his hand. There was no way not to stop, and he brought the car to the side and wound down the window.

"Good morning," he called, and was annoyed that there was that audible flaw in his voice again. Corder came up, looking large in his shooting coat.

"Good morning, Mr. Fleming."

"You're early."

"I've been shooting my lunch," said Corder with a smile. He slapped the birds lightly against his thigh. "Looks like a great day."

"I wish I didn't have to spend it in my office." Denis laughed but again it lacked conviction.

He drove on, winding up the window and thinking of Corder's open face and powerful physique. It would never be possible to strangle Corder, he thought. Not the way you strangle a puppy.

Denis had been at his desk for about two hours when Colonel Ferris telephoned. His voice was clipped, authoritarian. "I'd like you to call."

"Can you tell me what sort of job it is, Colonel, then I'll know who to send. If it's trouble with your television, then I'll have a man in that area this afternoon."

"I wish you to call personally, Mr. Fleming." He hesitated. "I should tell you that it's a confidential matter."

Denis turned over the pages of his desk diary. "What

about Friday at three thirty . . . or anytime Friday afternoon?"

"I'd rather hoped you could come sooner. It's fairly
important."

In the silence while he turned pages again Denis
could hear dogs barking in the Colonel's house. "I could
call sometime about midday today but I'm not sure exactly
when it will be."

"That would suit very well. I'll look out for you."

Denis replaced the receiver and wrote the Colonel's
name neatly in the diary. He added a question mark
automatically, before returning to the open ledger on his
desk. There was a slight distortion in his vision, he noticed
as he wrote, which seemed to move with his eyes. It was
like the diagrammatic structure of some atomic particle.
He blinked several times but it didn't go away and after a
few minutes, as work absorbed him, he ceased to notice it.

At eleven Rosemary brought his coffee and when
she'd gone he took two cookies from the tin which he
kept in his desk and walked to the window nibbling them.
Below in the Market Square a police car drove up to the
Guild Hall, scattering the pigeons, and he remembered
that today was a day when the magistrates sat. The Colonel
was frequently on the bench, he remembered, too.

Denis went back to his desk to unhook the rather
severe steel-rimmed spectacles he wore for close work and
to slide on the executive pair that he believed impressed
his customers more. He went downstairs to the workshop,
past the row of television sets on the test bench, to where
Barney was checking a chassis with an ammeter. A pop
group were whispering the words of "Gone Baby," against
a background of bells, and one of the apprentices turned
the volume down deferentially.

Denis said, "I'm going out to Wickham Market . . . to the Ferris place."

"There's a service truck just back."

"I'll take my own car. I shan't come in again before lunch."

Barney nodded, and Denis went on again to open a locker where he kept his personal tool kit. As he went out through the showroom, Rosemary was bent over the counter with a customer fitting batteries to a clock. Denis drove west onto the bypass and when he was cruising comfortably he punched the radio switch. "Gone Baby" was just finishing. He wondered if Louise was listening to it and, remembering her, he was visited by a feeling of anxiety.

He'd left the document case on his desk unlocked with the tape still in it. Although he knew it was totally irrational, he tried to conceive of circumstances in which someone might take it. A thief, perhaps, while the shop was empty during the lunch hour. His mouth dried up as he thought about it. Or Barney going up for something and accidentally knocking the case off the desk. The contents spilled, Barney bends to pick up the tape curiously. . . . For a moment Denis considered going back, but now there wasn't time. He groaned out loud and pinched his moustache until it hurt.

He turned right past the church at Wickham Market and followed a narrow lane lined with hazel until he reached the triangular green. The gas station and Red Lion Hotel were on two sides of it, and on the other the Ferrises' Georgian residence sat half a mile back from the road. Denis drove through the open white gates and across a cattle grid into parkland. Floods had eroded the Colonel's drive and he shifted down as the car bounced over potholes. Then as he circled the enormous spread of a cedar of Lebanon he saw the Colonel waiting by the steps.

The Colonel moved swiftly out into the path of the car, and as Denis braked he came up to the window. "Hello, Fleming . . . would you mind parking at the side there? My wife's expecting people for luncheon." As Denis backed and drove down toward the stables, he walked beside the open window. "That will do," he said when they were out of sight of the front. Denis switched off the engine and climbed out.

The Colonel was already moving away. "Let's go straight in," he said over his shoulder.

He was one of the new breed of colonels, hard, cool, and with a close-cropped head, and he was rich enough to have retired in his early forties. They said in the village that the money was his wife's. He wore a deep-skirted hacking jacket with leather-patched sleeves. As he went up the steps ahead of Denis he said, "Glass is falling, looks as if there's rain on the way."

Denis didn't answer, and they passed into a large, bright hallway. He could smell the Colonel's toilet water as sharp as a frosty morning. The door to the right opened into a morning room where a fire flickered in an Adam fireplace.

Ferris called, "We shan't be long," and continued on up the carpeted stairs. No one answered.

When they reached the upstairs landing the Colonel opened double doors into the long room facing north. He snapped several switches by the door, and a dozen or so picture lights came to muted life.

"You've been here before, of course."

"We had the contract for the installation. It was a year ago."

"But you've never seen the pictures?" The Colonel

walked ahead of him, and Denis at his shoulder felt as if he were reviewing a guard of honor. They passed dark landscapes, reminiscent of Constable.

"Croome you know, of course . . . he's enjoying a certain vogue at the moment . . . and Hardwick. . . ." They wheeled at the end of the long gallery and stopped before the Flemish portrait of a nobleman.

"Van Dyck," said the Colonel crisply. "Supposed to be an ancestor of my wife's. The collection's part of an inheritance."

They moved back by the windows. Denis could see a boy of about nine, idling, playing with a rope that hung from a branch of the cedar. He looked pale and overdressed. Then the Colonel saw him also.

"That's my youngest. His prep school goes back rather late. Always hanging around . . . doesn't seem able to amuse himself." He moved as though to open the window and then changed his mind. "Little devil doesn't realize how lucky he is to be in the country. He could be playing in the street with a crowd of yobbos." Then he added, "I don't mean Woodbridge, of course."

Denis said, "I don't live in Woodbridge."

"No, of course not." Ferris moved on. "These two drawings are by Rembrandt . . . part of a series he did for one of the Durgher paintings."

They were back by the door. Denis looked around again. "I imagine they're quite valuable."

"That is why I asked you here. The insurance company insists we have an up-to-date security system before they'll renew the policy. They say you're one of their approved installers for this area."

"We've done one or two, but nothing elaborate. Some of the rooms at the Ipswich Museum. . . ."

"What is the form exactly?"

"It comes complete from Steinitz Systems of Coventry
—they're a German subsidiary. I'll send you a catalog if
you wish."

"I'd rather you told me."

"Well, it's a series of contact switches in a ringed circuit that goes through all the windows and doors, and the
pictures themselves if you wanted. Then a secondary series
of vibrator switches that can be fitted in the walls and
floors, for instance. There are also electronic microscanners
across the room in case anyone manages to bypass either of
the other circuits. It's guaranteed as an alarm system but
not, of course, as fully protective."

The Colonel smiled coolly. "Don't worry, as long as
the alarm goes off I have the means of supplying the pro-
tection myself. How much does it cost?" As Denis hesitated, he added, "Very roughly. I shan't hold you to it."

"In the region of two hundred pounds. There are
cheaper systems, I believe. . . ."

"No, I like the sound of that."

Downstairs they heard quick running footsteps and
someone called, "Darling!" A car door slammed distantly.

Colonel Ferris moved to the door. "How soon can it
be done?"

"We could start next Tuesday. Three days should be
long enough."

"Right. Put it in hand, will you." Ferris pushed up
the switches and led the way out onto the landing. They
went down the first flight, and as they rounded the post
there were people in the hall below just entering the morning room on the left. The Colonel paused, waiting for
them to disappear.

He smiled briefly at Denis. "No point in getting involved in explanations." As they went on down he added, "In any case, I expect the matter to be treated as confidential."

"Naturally. Would you like me to send you a detailed estimate?"

"No need." They stopped as a blond woman came out of the doorway and caught sight of them. She was wearing a short dress of amber wool, with green beads that reached to her waist. Stella Ferris smiled at her husband. It was the smile of a predator, with deep lines etched at the corners of her mouth.

She said, "Bunty and James are here. Are you nearly through?"

"Mr. Fleming's just leaving."

Denis said, "I can find my own way out."

She looked at him for the first time. "Of course . . . Mr. Fleming from Market Square." She turned to her husband. "You go and do your stuff with the guests, darling. I'll show Mr. Fleming out."

Colonel Ferris hesitated. "Right," he said. "Thank you for coming so promptly, Fleming."

As he turned away, Mrs. Ferris said, "This way, Mr. Fleming," and led him off down a side passage. They reached a door that had hideous glass panels, and she stopped suddenly and turned. "I nearly forgot. . . . There was something I wanted to ask you."

"Yes?"

"I gave a lift to a man the other day who said he was renting a cottage from you. Can you tell me where it is? And his name?"

Denis blinked. "I . . . er, think his name is Corder. Yes, Corder. The cottage is next to our house . . . on the other side of Easton."

After a short silence Mrs. Ferris said with a rush, "I only asked because he said he was interested in shooting. My husband is sometimes short of a gun during the week. I'll drop him a line." She opened the door, saying, "Goodbye, Mr. Fleming."

"Goodbye."

Denis walked out onto the driveway at the side of the house and heard the door close behind him. The boy was standing beside his car, staring fixedly at the dashboard. He turned at the sound of Denis's step on the gravel, and there was a flash of anxiety in his eyes.

When Denis smiled at him he didn't smile back. Denis said, "It's a French car. Have you seen one before?"

The boy said, "No, sir," in a breathless, piping voice. Denis climbed in and started it up, then drew off in a wide curve back to the drive again. As he accelerated away, he could see the small figure still motionless in the rearview mirror.

Denis closed his eyes suddenly against the reflection of a childhood he had known himself.

[2]

.

Corder, reaching for a fine brush, noticed the letter again where he had propped it against an empty flowerpot on the mantelpiece.

It had been there all day, ever since Corder had picked it up with his milk on the way back from his morning shoot. It was addressed to James Wallace, Burdock Cottage, Easton, Nr. Woodbridge. Corder swore quietly as he worked. He was working from colored photographs, but even so it was difficult to get the real charm of the vole, which was more like a baby bear or maybe a beaver than a rat. What he needed was a cage trap so he could watch it for a while. But what could he bait it with? Voles were herbivorous. They had all the grass and leaves they wanted around the pond. Maybe a late autumn apple would tempt him? He'd ask them down at the pub. Someone might know. As he stepped back, he was aware of the letter again.

It was an airmail letter that had been mailed in Australia a week ago. What he really ought to do was to take it up to the house and give it to Mrs. Fleming and say, "Here's a letter for the previous tenant, and what did you mean you hadn't really rented the cottage before?"

Maybe she had just forgotten . . . which was nothing to make a fuss about. But what the hell was a brand-new funeral urn doing in the garden? Corder put his brush between his teeth and went over to pick up the letter. The back flap was slightly torn where he'd started to open it and stopped. Then suddenly his thumb was under it, and he'd torn it open. It was a single sheet covered on one side with an angular scrawl.

Dear Jim,

Your letter only reached me a week ago. It was re-addressed from the barracks in Colchester because some clot in the army P.O. hadn't put on any more postage and it came out sea mail.

Anyway it certainly threw me! God knows what will have happened by the time you get this, but if I were you I'd pack my bags and get out fast! Otherwise there could be big, big trouble. Remember Kathleen? Why don't you come out here? The climate's fair, the natives are friendly, and there's plenty of work. Anyway your trade is in demand wherever you go! Write soon and let me know you are still in the land of the living, otherwise I shall worry about you. Yours, Jeff

Corder read it twice, then put it carefully back in the envelope and smoothed it. Now, too late, he wished he'd left the bloody thing alone. Because now he was going to worry what big, big trouble the previous tenant might have got into. The stupid thing was that he might all the time be worrying unnecessarily. The expression *pack your bags and get out fast* could possibly be metaphorical and could be referring to any kind of personal situation . . . or even a business situation. Corder wondered, in passing, what essential work it was that Wallace had performed. He decided to ask them in the pub.

He lifted his head suddenly at the sound of a car stopping somewhere out on the driveway.

Denis signed his mail at five fifteen and afterward he filled in the order form for Steinitz Systems. When Rosemary came for the mail at five thirty, something stopped his hand as he was passing over the Steinitz envelope.

"It needn't go now. I may have something to add."

"See you tomorrow then, Mr. Fleming."

The door banged, and he sat there frozen, aware that a step had been taken but not yet understanding what it was.

He had kept the order form back because he had decided to order two of the systems. He didn't know why, it wasn't really necessary to have one in stock, but the meaningless gesture had been both impulsive and compulsive. He took off his glasses and rubbed rhythmically at the lenses.

Below in the workshop the pop music had died away, and he heard the doors slamming as the staff left. Only Barney would be there now. Denis felt irritated with Barney who never left early, who would be fiddling around for half an hour yet, making out time sheets and checking the order book. Two years ago, after Louise's operation and when it was certain he would have no heir, he had given Barney a small percentage of the business.

Denis opened a drawer halfway down his desk. The tape was lying there. He picked it up and put it down, then snapped the drawer shut again. It would be an hour before he knew.

As he left the desk and went to the window, he heard the flat sound of the mechanic's scooter starting up and revving, like distant static, and then a moment later it flashed by below him and careered away out of sight. The parking lot was emptying slowly, and the florist opposite was carrying his sidewalk display back into the shop. Denis moved on to where the tape deck had been built into the shelves. He flicked it on and waited while the circuit warmed and the monitor lights swam slowly into focus. When he clicked it off again, he was aware that his hand was shaking slightly. He turned suddenly and went out onto the landing.

Below in the workshop the strip lights were off, and Barney was working under a desk lamp at the bench. Denis saw that he was filling in the job numbers from the mechanic's worksheets.

"You work too hard, Barney." He tried to make his voice sound light.

"Somebody has to, Mr. Fleming. All these young buggers think about is rushing off to meet their birds."

"You should get a bird yourself." Too late he remembered that Barney's wife had been killed in a car crash and that he was living with his shrewish, violent mother. Out of the sticky silence came the sound of voices from the shop.

Denis turned his head and looked at his watch. "I

thought Rosemary had gone," he said, and walked through. The display lighting was still on, and Rosemary was facing a young man in a leather jacket, who had close-cropped hair. Beyond, in the doorway, a girl in a raincoat waited mutely.

Rosemary turned as soon as he came in. "It's Mr. Tucker," she said. "He's called about the payments."

"How many weeks do they owe?"

"It was just four weeks yesterday."

"I'm sorry, Mr. Fleming," Tucker said calmly, "I just haven't got it."

"Then you shouldn't have bought the set."

"I've been laid off. They're cutting down for the winter."

The spit crackled quietly in the background.

"I'll deal with it, Rosemary. You can go home."

"All right, Mr. Fleming." She picked up her bag and library book and went out. Denis moved behind the counter.

"All right. I'll have the truck pick it up tomorrow."

The girl said clearly, "Before four?"

Tucker added, "We'd appreciate it if they could call before four o'clock."

"You mean before the neighbors get home from work," said Denis wearily.

Tucker looked at him steadily. "No, Mr. Fleming, I don't care about the neighbors. I mean before the kids get home from school. I don't want it taken away when they're in the house."

Denis looked down at the book, opened at the Tucker account. They'd paid a twenty percent deposit and been making payments for three months. He closed the book and moved away.

"We're rather pushed for storage at the moment . . .

in fact I'd rather not take it in just now. Come and see me in six weeks, or sooner if you get another job."

"I'd rather not, Mr. Fleming."

Denis turned off the main showroom lighting, leaving just the window display. The light from the spit seemed to splash on the darkened ceiling. "You'd be obliging me," he said. "I'd rather have the money later than be stuck with a secondhand set."

Tucker still hesitated. "I don't know what to say, Mr. Fleming. . . ."

"I'm afraid I must turn you out. We should have been closed twenty minutes ago."

Tucker was retreating at last. "I shan't forget it, Mr. Fleming. . . ."

After the door closed, Denis opened the cash book again and made a note against the account. As he shut the book, he was aware of Barney watching him from the workshop door.

"I heard you at it again, Mr. Fleming."

"It's not really his fault, Barney. We'll make it up somewhere else."

"We can't keep running the business on the Robin Hood principle. We didn't make the world the way it is."

"No, but we have to live in it."

He moved past Barney back into the workshop. "It's good for our reputation. . . . Might even bring in business."

"The sort we don't want. Everyone in the district who knows you're a soft touch."

Denis looked at his watch. It was after six. How much longer, he thought bitterly. Aloud he said, "Haven't you finished, Barney?"

"Shan't be long. I'm on the last sheet."

Denis turned away, almost shaking. "Go away, damn you," his mind was shouting. "For Christ's sake go away and leave me alone!" But again, aloud, he only said, "I've a few things to clear up myself."

He went upstairs again.

The square was almost empty now and the sky was red in the west.

He reached up and drew the curtains carefully, and as he turned, he heard Barney moving at last. The door of the locker closed, and then footsteps came back toward the stairs.

"Good night, Mr. Fleming," he called. "I'll lock up as I go."

"Goodbye, Barney."

He waited until the workshop door closed and then the side door, then he switched on the desk lamp. He was alone at last. . . .

Not *really* alone, he thought pedantically, not really alone. . . .

He picked up the tape from the drawer and carried it across to the tape deck. He threaded it carefully, ran off the first few inches, and then pressed the hold button. He moved away to the mirror and, taking a comb from his vest pocket, carefully recombed his hair. The round, sad face with the spectacles and the bristle moustache seemed in a way to belong to someone else.

"A drink," he whispered to his reflection. He opened another drawer of the desk, where a glass and bottle were wrapped in a hand towel. He half-filled the glass and put the bottle back. "Ready," he said, out loud again. He could have been a man preparing to receive guests.

He pressed the fast-run switch on the deck and the tape sped by, silent except for the regular high-pitched tinkle of the clock chimes. Then, when the gabbled voices began, he stopped it and ran it back a little. He started it again at the normal speed and returned to his desk, carrying the glass. The speakers came alive suddenly with the distant sounds of car brakes, and somewhere in the house a door slammed.

Her footsteps sounded abruptly on the parquet floor of the living room and bolts rattled at the french window.

Louise cried, "Darling!"

There was silence for several moments before the voice of Colonel Ferris said, "Hello, sweetie . . . you look ravishing as usual."

"Well, after all, I expect to be ravished." They laughed together.

Then Louise said, "Will you have a whisky?"

"Yes, please . . . but just a small one."

Glasses tinkled against the decanter, and Ferris crossed to sit down heavily on the chaise. Denis heard his shoes fall one by one as he kicked them off. He spoke lazily. "I'm giving your husband some useful employment shortly."

Louise must also have removed her shoes, because although he never heard her footsteps come back she began speaking from close by. "In what way?"

"I'm having him install a burglar alarm in the gallery. I hope to get him up tomorrow."

Then Louise said drily, "It's rather amusing to think of him installing a burglar alarm there while you're breaking in here." Ferris laughed again, and there was a sound of drinking before Louise added, "Let me put my legs inside. . . ."

Denis spread his hands on the desk pad and closed his eyes. Although there hadn't been much time, he'd hoped that yesterday her lover might have been Corder. He sat there frowning, oblivious to the sound track. Now that he knew it wasn't Corder he was no longer interested. What was *wrong.* . . .

He was roused later by the snapping of a lighter. Louise said, "What's wrong?" as if she was echoing his thought.

"There was somebody in the cottage garden when I drove up. I don't know whether he knew me."

"He doesn't. He's the new tenant. He's quite harmless."

"Who is he?"

"Oh, an American painter . . . he's taken it for the winter. He's also a shooting man, McDougall has given him the run of the wood."

"Let's hope he's discreet."

"I should say he's supremely uninterested. He keeps himself to himself."

She must have moved because Ferris said, "Don't go . . . I want to tell you something amusing about Stella."

"Last time you were here you told me something amusing about Stella. When you come here I don't particularly want to hear amusing things about Stella." She'd pushed her feet into her shoes and they rat-tatted around before she crossed to the sideboard. The glasses rang as she put them down.

Nearer at hand, Ferris sighed resignedly and began to dress. "When shall I see you again?"

"I'm not sure." She stayed speaking from a distance. "It can't be tomorrow or Thursday. Why don't you call me Friday."

"Friday doesn't suit me. I've got a meeting of the Conservancy Board."

"Then it'll have to be next week."

"You don't seem to care too much."

Her footsteps came back slowly, and there was momentary silence. Then she said, "That's how much I care. Now try and understand."

"Now you've made me all excited again."

"Well, that's too bad . . . I'm late already. Say goodbye nicely, then I'm going up to change." Then a moment later, in alarm, she said, "Darling, *please*. . . ." Her footsteps ran away. "Friday at the usual time," she said before the door closed.

Money chinked in a pocket as Ferris finished dressing; then he crossed the room, humming softly. The french window opened and closed. As Ferris's car started and revved up, Denis punched the rewind button. Then he went back to the desk and got a carton. He hesitated for a moment and then filled in the label with a ball-point pen, printing the words carefully. "Colonel Ferris, 19 September." Then when the tape ran clear he took it from the deck and put it in the box.

He bent down to a cabinet below the tape deck and unlocked it with a key from his wallet. There were between fifty and sixty tapes on the shelf, going back long before Ferris. He added the latest one to the stack and closed the door again.

He was still thinking about Corder. "I'll have to do something," he said out loud.

His head had begun to ache abominably. It was as if his brain had somehow assumed the characteristics of his heart and had become a great pumping muscle.

[3]

Corder opened the door and found himself facing Stella Ferris.

She said, "Good evening, Mr. Corder."

Corder said, "Hello," and smiled. He stepped away, holding the door open, and she went by.

"You see I know your name."

"And where I live!"

"Well, I haven't been spying, if that's what you think. It just happens that I met Mr. Fleming and he told me."

She was wearing caterpillar boots and a straight skirt of Donegal tweed. Over a tan sweater she wore a sleeveless cardigan of raw, untreated wool. She stood in front of the easel with her legs apart. "I like your vole very much," she said. "Does it live in that pond?"

"Yes. There may be a pair of them."

She turned to face him. "They live very immoral lives, you know. Females overlap the males, so to speak."

"I didn't know that," Corder said.

"Speaking territorially as well as sexually. The British Mammal Society published an amusing paper about them last year. My husband's a Fellow."

She moved away again, and put one leg on the bottom stair, looking up.

"Are you alone here?"

Corder didn't know why he hesitated. "Well . . . yes."

She looked at him with her cool gray eyes and a faint smile. He noticed again the deep creases in her cheeks where the smile ended. Corder knew what was in the air, and now was the time for him to make some ambiguous remark. He waited through a long silence before he said, "Would you like a cup of tea?"

"No, thank you, but I wouldn't mind a drink."

"I'm afraid I've only whisky."

"But I love whisky."

He went out to the kitchen and took down the bottle and a couple of glasses from the cupboard. When he went back, she was sitting at the end of the settee with her legs crossed.

He said, "I only have water to put with it."

"Thank you, I prefer it plain." And while he poured and gave it to her she said, "I came up because I remembered about the shooting."

"Oh yes."

"Today I happened to see Mr. Fleming, the little man with the radio shop, and he told me you were here. I've spoken to my husband, and he often has room in the gun line. We charge ten pounds a day, by the way. Beaters and good dogs are quite difficult to get hold of, and of course we provide you with a loader."

Corder sipped his whisky in silence.

"I'm quite a good loader myself," she said, smiling at him again. "I often stand with my husband. We've got a shoot organized next Tuesday."

"I can't come on Tuesday," Corder said firmly. "I should tell you I've already fixed myself up with some rough shooting."

Again there was a silence. Stella Ferris turned the whisky in her glass thoughtfully. "I should have called sooner."

When Corder still didn't speak she drained her whisky suddenly and stood up. "Well, if you feel like it later in the month, or if anything goes wrong with your present arrangement, you can give me a ring. My telephone number is in the book." She moved to stand in front of him with one hand pushed forward on her hip. "Goodbye, Mr. Corder."

Corder turned away to put his glass down. "Thanks a lot for letting me know about the shoot." He went to open the door and stood aside for her.

"Don't bother to come out," she said.

"No bother at all." Corder went ahead of her down the path and through the rose bed. As he opened the door of the MG for her, another car came sweeping up the drive. Corder waved automatically and Denis Fleming waved back without slowing or turning his head.

Stella Ferris slid in behind the wheel and started the engine. She glanced up at him, turned her smile on and off briefly, and then was gone in a scatter of stones.

After Denis had put the car away, he left his case on the front steps and walked out across the lawn in the dusk.

He stood for a while between two of the herbaceous beds, looking back at the house. Almost unconsciously he was screwing a fist into the palm of one hand. Then he saw Louise open the kitchen window and wave to him. He waved back vaguely before walking on between the Michaelmas daisies and the last remnants of roses. Distantly he heard the Ferris car drive off, honking loudly before it turned into the lane.

There was another Suffolk sunset, the color of a blood orange, and a distant flight of Phantoms was descending through the peaceful sky toward the Bentwaters strip. At the end of the walk there was a sundial with an ornate grass gnomon, which he'd bought from a country-house sale. With irritation, Denis saw that moles had been burrowing all around it. There were several hills and some long shallow runs. He kicked with sudden abandon at the first molehill and nearly fell over. He recovered quickly and started again, hacking with both feet.

"Bastards!" he kept saying, under his breath. "Bastards! Bastards! Bastards!" He began running with short steps, up and down the runs, stamping them flat. He reached another molehill and was smashing it down, almost in a frenzy, when Louise called from the front of the house.

"Darling? Aren't you coming in?"

His panted breath was white in the cold air. "Just coming." He smoothed the last molehill away more slowly with his foot and then started back toward the house.

She was waiting for him on the steps. As he came up she said, "What a lovely sky."

"There's a bloody mole wrecking the lawn again!" He walked past her into the hallway and put down his case.

Louise followed slowly, watching his rigid back. She said, "Let's have a drink. I've been looking forward to one all the time I've been cooking."

Denis opened the door and crossed the living room to the liquor cabinet. Bottles and glasses rattled noisily as he moved them around searching for the malt whisky.

"What would you like?"

"A martini—very dry. With lots of gin. I'll get some ice."

When she came back with it, he had left her drink on the sideboard and was standing in the long window with his own, watching the sky. As she looked at him she could see that his hand by his side was trembling faintly.

She said, "I'd expected you to be in a good mood tonight. A very good mood."

Denis gulped his drink and went back to the cabinet again.

Louise said, "Won't you tell me what's wrong?"

"I saw the Ferris car parked down at the cottage."

Louise's eyes opened fractionally. "When?"

"This evening, when I came home."

The Westminster chimes rang softly through the room. Then Louise said calmly, "I suppose there's no reason why Colonel Ferris shouldn't call on. . . ."

"Not *Colonel* Ferris. *Mrs.*"

"Oh."

Denis went back to the window. The tip of his finger moved restlessly to and fro across the stubble of his moustache. "It's not right," he whispered. "Not right at all. It's the scandal, apart from anything else. . . . If . . . she's carrying on with him."

"You don't *know* that. . . ."

Denis went on as if she hadn't spoken. "And another thing . . . Colonel Ferris is a client of the firm."

The ice chinked in Louise's drink as she sipped it. There was no other sound in the room. He turned his head to look at her steadily. "That's not what we rented him the cottage for. Why don't you go down and see him tomorrow."

"All right, I will."

It was almost dark when Corder left the cottage and walked across the grass, skirting the rose bed.

He heard a plop as the vole dropped into the pond and the nervous ticking of a moorhen from the direction of the willows. The sky was still flushed as he set off down the drive, making for the pub. When he came out into the lane, the lights of the village were visible.

There was no one in the bar except Cooker, an elderly, gnarled man who was dozing in a corner. When Nell came slopping through from the kitchen, Corder ordered beer from the barrel. "Join me," he added.

"I couldn't. I've just had my tea."

She pushed the hair away from her open face. Her freckled skin looked moist and translucent. She said, "They say on telly there'll be rain before morning. Have you been shooting?"

"I was out for an hour. Shot a brace of pigeons." He put his glass down carefully. "Tell me something . . . the man who used to rent the place before . . . you've never heard where he might have gone? Or would you know if anyone's seen him?"

"No, he just upped and went, the way I told you. It was Mr. Fleming told someone he owed rent."

A red setter came into the bar behind the counter, its tail swishing. It put its paws up opposite Corder, and Nell said, "Down, Rover," mechanically, but the dog stayed there, watching Corder with sad intelligence.

"*He* had a little cat for company."

"Who did?"

"The man who used to live at Burdock Cottage. He was very fond of his little cat . . . often had a bit of fish for it if he called in on his way home."

"What kind of work did he do?"

"I don't rightly know. Something over Woodbridge way."

When Louise Fleming walked down the drive she saw that the Land-Rover was missing from alongside the garage. She went idly on until she came to the lane. Opposite the drive sycamores were growing, and she picked her way through them into a newly plowed field. The sun was bright but cool through the haze. A cock pheasant got up, almost from under her feet, and went rocketing away across the chocolate-brown furrows. She chose a mound on the edge of the field and sat down to wait.

It was twenty minutes before the Land-Rover came back. She heard the rasp of gears as it shifted down to enter the drive. She stood up and started walking back down the furrow to the sycamores. When she came out of the trees, the Land-Rover was parked in its usual place, and the front door of the cottage was open. She was nervous and forced herself to walk slowly.

Corder had unpacked his duffel bag in the kitchen and eaten a bowl of cornflakes before going back to his painting. He had taken down yesterday's board and put up another with half a dozen colored photographs tacked along the top of it. They were all of the vole swimming, with its nose and beady eyes just breaking the surface of the water. He picked up a pencil and started to block out the shape. Stella Ferris had surprised him yesterday with her knowledge of voles. He'd like to have heard more about that society she'd spoken of.

It was a pity, Corder thought, that painters were always a target for women who were bored and randy. He blamed it all on the wicked French Impressionists, some of whom had been men of more than easy virtue. It was then that he heard Louise Fleming's step and saw her shadow in the doorway.

"May I come in?"

He said, "Surely," but didn't move away from the easel. He smiled. "What can I do for you, Mrs. Fleming?"

She moved slowly down the far wall opposite him and leaned a hip against the settee. She said, "Well, nothing really . . . I was just out for a walk and saw your door open."

Corder turned back to the easel with a sinking heart. All the signs of the schoolmistressy woman who'd shown him the cottage were gone; instead her hair was loose and she was bursting her way out of a shirt dress. In fact she looked quite attractive, more than he'd have thought possible, and he could tell from her manner that she was trying to show it to him.

"I thought I'd make sure you were settled in . . . that there was nothing you needed."

"Nothing," he said. "Everything's fine, and I'm very comfortable." He turned away deliberately to pick up an eraser and shorten a line.

As he blew the board clean she said, "I heard you shooting in the woods."

More silence.

"Have you had any partridge?"

"I had one yesterday . . . out in the corn stubble."

"They're mostly French ones around here, people say . . . with red bottoms."

Corder picked up his pencil again. "I'm sure you won't mind if I get on with this. I've been working at it for days, and this morning for the first time I seem to be getting it right."

"I don't mind," she said. "Would you like me to make you some coffee or tea or whatever you have?"

"No thanks. I've just had breakfast. You make some if you'd like it, though."

Corder hummed quietly under his breath as he worked, trying to give an impression of deep concentration. He heard her move further behind him and the springs of the settee squeak, and when he looked around she was curled in it, showing rather a lot of leg.

She caught his eye and smiled. "You don't mind if I just sit here and watch, do you? It's one of those days when I can't settle to anything in the house."

"I don't mind." Corder picked up a magnifying glass to look closely at one of the photographs. It was a very curious thing that a vole seemed to wrinkle its nose along the top while it was swimming, almost as if it was following a scent. He studied two other photographs in turn.

Behind him Louise Fleming said softly, "You know you're very lucky not to be married."

"Mmmmm."

"It's the most frightful gamble, you know. Sometimes people don't get on at all."

Corder knew it as well as a litany. Now his response was that he was sorry she didn't get on with her husband. He couldn't help being conscious of the excitement in her voice. With only the faintest irony, he said, "I suppose you and your husband don't get on, Mrs. Fleming."

"But we do get on! We get on marvelously! We have the most super marriage." There was a short silence before she added, "Except for the physical side, of course. That's why we haven't any children."

Corder heard her stir and start to rearrange herself on the settee, but he deliberately didn't look around. When she spoke again her voice came from a slightly different direction.

"Oh! You're drawing one of those horrid water rats. . . ."

"It's a water vole, Mrs. Fleming."

"I saw one swim across the pond once. Denis . . . my husband, says they take the young mallard in the spring."

"They don't eat young mallard," said Corder patiently, "because they don't eat flesh."

It would almost be worth laying Mrs. Fleming, Corder thought bitterly, just to shut her up. At the same time he realized uneasily that she was beginning to get to him a little. The conflict about the voles had started the first, faint flicker of sexuality. Conflict was the fuel that a lot of marriages ran on, including that of Lou and Connie Voss. Corder did some rubbing out and then stepped away to look at the drawing through narrowed eyes.

Louise Fleming said, "Let me look," and stood up.

Unlike most painters, Corder didn't mind people looking at his work in the making, maybe because he felt it wasn't truly creative anyway. Like Walter Savage Landor he really loved nature most, and art came a poor second. In a way he was prepared for what happened next because it was a common part of the courtship routine, but what he wasn't prepared for was his own response. Louise Fleming stepped back a pace until her buttocks were lightly pressing his pelvis. He tried to step farther away himself, but he was against the round table. Then she was pressing him harder.

Corder said, "Hey look . . ." and his hands went down to her waist to move her away, but immediately she caught his wrists and took his hands around her so that they were covering her breasts.

Corder could feel her nipples as hard as bullets. He tried to move his hands away and in fact to step right out of it, but even as he did it he was aware that his arousal point had been reached and that the mercury was still going up.

"Take it easy!" he half-shouted. "It's crazy . . . you and I don't want to be mixed up like this. Oh Jesus. . . ."

Louise Fleming had twisted suddenly to face him but he turned his face away from her damp searching lips. But she kept his arms locked under hers, and her pelvis was driving against his. After a moment his hands were holding her of their own volition.

"Oh Jesus . . ." he said again weakly. And then her lips had covered his. Butterflies seemed to scorch his mouth.

They wrestled around for another five minutes before Corder said, "Okay . . . upstairs," in a voice that wasn't quite steady.

"No."

Corder thought: Oh, Christ, not one of *those*. He grabbed her wrist. But he'd only gone a pace before she'd twisted free and was facing him. She was panting,

95

voluptuous, and unbuttoned, and she reminded Corder of someone out of a very bad movie.

"Come up to the house in five minutes," she whispered tensely. "It's better."

"But what if your husband . . ."

"He never comes back. *Never!*"

"I don't . . ."

"Please," she said urgently.

"Okay."

Then she was running away across the rose bed. He watched her dart through the wicket gate and turn up the drive. He said "Bloody hell," out loud and looked down at the floor. He found the pencil lying where he'd dropped it, and he picked it up and dropped it back in the flower-pot with the others. He knew it was crazy to get involved with her, but the trouble was the genie was out of the bottle now and it wasn't going back until it had what it wanted.

He went out of the house and down the path. At the gate he hesitated again, cursing himself. He knew it was a plumb crazy situation, that sooner or later all he would have was big, big trouble. Big, big trouble . . . the phrase from Wallace's letter seemed to force its way into his mind.

He turned suddenly, ran across to the Land-Rover and climbed in. He thumped the wheel. "Bloody hell," he said again, angrily. He started the engine.

Louise Fleming heard the sound of the Land-Rover engine starting up and revving. She was lying naked on the chaise beside the french window. She closed her eyes.

She heard it back away from the garage and then accelerate swiftly. She opened her eyes again as it stopped outside and Corder's footsteps crushed the gravel. He stepped into the room.

"I thought you were never coming," she said.

And after a moment, when he was kneeling beside her, she murmured, "Puppykins. . . ."

Corder thought that he knew all the diminutives of love, but *Puppykins.* . . . "For Christ's sake," he whispered, "why call me. . . ." He couldn't finish. He couldn't finish because suddenly his mouth seemed to be full of hers.

PART
III

[1]

Corder didn't know what woke him, just that his eyes were open in the dark. The sou'wester which had been blowing all the previous day had died away, and the night was still. He threw back the covers and crossed to the bathroom, moving with confidence, for it was now November and he'd been in residence five weeks. After he'd peed noisily and flushed it away he ran lightly downstairs to check that the paraffin stove wasn't smoking. On the way back to bed he glanced out the window and noticed a light burning up at Burdock House.

The first time Corder had been awakened at night

had been about ten days before and he'd thought at first it was the voice of a woman singing, a song full of sustained melancholy. He had heard it on the edge of consciousness, rising and falling for some time, and it seemed to be coming from the woods behind the house.

It was only when he roused himself that he realized it was the yowling of a cat.

He'd heard it three or four times since, always at night, and he often wondered if it was Wallace's cat, if Wallace had gone off in such a hurry that he had left it behind, and now it was living wild in the woods. But he thought he would have seen it, or at least traces of it. Corder turned on his side and closed his eyes. On another night he'd heard a dog fox barking far off in the woods east of the village. There were fewer foxes now, the old men in the pub had told him, since myxomatosis had killed off the rabbits. Then Corder heard again the sound which he knew must have awakened him—the long throbbing mew of the little owl. He knew it was in the pear tree by the pond because he found its droppings under the branches every morning.

Corder turned restlessly and wondered which of them was awake up at Burdock House. Or even, wryly, if they were both awake and making love. On the whole he thought not. At the start, after he'd made love to Louise for the first time, he'd spent two anxious days kicking himself. It was an old bachelor's maxim that you didn't foul your own doorstep. Corder was well aware of the complications it could give rise to, and they could even be legal if Fleming ever found out. But it hadn't happened like that at all. Louise Fleming was just a good old-fashioned sensualist whose husband was underpowered. She probably loved him, for it turned out that she had

just the same horror as he did of any emotional involve-
ment. Corder smiled in the dark as he thought for the
hundredth time that he really had the perfect arrangement, a little sexual therapy once or twice a week with no
strings attached.

If she had hand-picked him she couldn't have chosen
a man who fitted better into her scheme of things. And
also for the hundredth time he wondered at the fantastic
coincidence that out of ten million people in London, he
should have been the first to see her advertisement in the
newspaper and call her up.

Corder ate half a cold pheasant for his tea the next
day before going out for a late shoot. The season had
ended in October, and it had been hanging in the larder
ever since. He had shot it running, what he called Ken-
tucky rules, which would have been enough to have had
him drummed out of the district if anyone had been
watching. But Corder excused himself on the grounds
that he was shooting strictly for the pot and that walking
them up on his own made it very difficult to get the birds
off the ground.

He hooked his field glasses around his neck and
stepped out into the late afternoon where the sun was
already a red ball. For a while he stood in the shelter of
the crack willows and searched the edge of the pond with
the glasses. It was two days since he'd seen the vole, and
he was as conscious of it as other people might have been
conscious of missing a meal. But there was no movement
around the run or among the reeds, and after a while he
moved off quietly past the house and up the path through
the woods. When he came out on the other side of them,
he paused and loaded up with two shells.

He moved on, slowly and silently, against the dark

background. Halfway to the lane, a brace of pigeons burst from a tree ahead of him, but they'd swerved away in the half-light before he had the gun steady.

He turned when he reached the lane and started to move back again. There was a fallow field on his left where sugar beet had been harvested and where the winter plowing hadn't yet been done. He stopped when he reached the end of it and spent a long time searching it carefully. When he was about to move on, the hare hopped out of cover about fifty yards away and stopped with its ears up. Corder waited, as frozen and watchful as the hare. After a moment it lolloped on a dozen steps and began feeding with its back to him. He moved the butt of the gun gently into his shoulder and waited. It was beyond range and a poor shot from the back. A hare was hard to kill and he remembered still the third hare he'd ever shot. It had been running across his front and his deflection had been poor so that he'd hit it too far back. It had crouched down with its legs broken and its ears flat, screaming like a woman. He'd been shooting with an old single-barrel, and he remembered the dreadful sound going on and on while he fumbled to reload.

A crow swept down on fringed wings, carrying something in its beak, and the hare stopped feeding and turned. It came hopping toward him. When it was thirty yards away he raised the gun and shot it cleanly in the head and forequarters. It rolled over, twitching. He unloaded the second barrel and went forward to pick it up, and as he did so he noticed the small nob on the first joint of the forefoot that told him it was still a leveret.

Just as he was about to reenter the shelter of the path Corder saw the white scut of a rabbit lying a little farther up the field. He went to look and saw it had been eaten away up to the rump. It was the first trace he'd seen of the cat. A fox would have eaten the whole carcass or just the guts, but a cat always left the back legs. He turned it over with his boot. It was still fresh.

He called, "Puss, puss," quietly, a dozen times, but nothing answered. As he went on again a flight of Phantoms roared over at about eight thousand feet in finger four formation, heading toward Woodbridge. They were lost in the darkening sky before the sound had faded. He came out behind the cottage and hung the hare temporarily on a galvanized hook with a plastic bowl underneath to catch the blood; then he went on to his stand under the crack willows. Again he searched the banks for signs of the vole, but there were only a couple of bluetits there fluttering among the dogwood stems.

Then something *did* move, down by the vole run, but it was a wren flitting along. He remembered then that at one time the British used to hunt the wren. He had once seen a print in a New York bookshop of burly men beating the bushes with clubs.

They were believed to be birds of ill omen.

The same jets that had passed over Easton peeled off in a landing pattern and sank screaming, one by one, over the Woodbridge rooftops. Denis had just combed his hair and was examining his moustache in the mirror. A glass of malt whisky was already standing on his desk pad. He turned his head away as he heard the slam of a locker door from the workroom below, and a moment later Barney's footsteps sounded on the first flight of stairs and stopped.

Barney called, "I'm off, Mr. Fleming. Good night."

"Good night, Barney."

The doors in the building slammed in succession, growing fainter, and then Denis saw him walking diagonally across the square up toward Theatre Street. Denis thought of the other, cruel half of life that waited for him there. Barney walked very straight, with measured steps, the way people would have walked to the scaffold.

He drew the curtains and went back to open and close the door automatically, but there was only darkness beyond it. Then, walking rather like Barney, he crossed the room to press the rapid-playback button. It ran for nearly half a minute before he heard the sound of garbled falsetto voices. He backtracked for twenty seconds, pressed the normal-speed playback, and returned to his chair. In the minute before the sound started he sipped his whisky and composed himself with his hands folded in his lap. Then the rat-tat-tat began of a coin on a glass panel of the french window.

It went on and on, regularly, like a drumbeat, until a door opened and Louise's footsteps hurried through. A key turned.

At a distance Corder said, "Hello, honey."

And then Louise: "I'm sorry . . . I thought it was unlocked." Then there was silence before she said, "Leave your coat outside."

"What for?"

"It smells of turpentine."

Then they were kissing, Denis knew, caressing. He took another mouthful of whisky and let it lie, tingling faintly, in his mouth.

As though he had prompted her, Louise's voice said suddenly: "Let's have a whisky."

"Okay. But I might tell you . . . I don't need any stimulation."

Louise laughed. A chink of glasses. Then somewhere close to the microphone Corder sat down and sighed. Louise said, "What have you been doing today?"

"Oh, I've been painting."

"Still those . . . whatever they are?"

"Water voles. No, I'm giving them a rest. Now the leaves are all down I've been painting birds. There's an old cock pheasant who roosts near the house every evening, I've been sketching him."

"What do you do with them all?"

"I just stack them away in my portfolio. There's a gallery on Fifth Avenue where they have a wildlife exhibition once in a while. They always show a few. Last year they made me all of one thousand dollars. I'm not really a financial success."

"But you don't need to be?"

"No, I don't need to be. I have my teaching. I'm comfortable."

Their conversation was muted, Denis thought, as though they were both conscious that whatever they said, the conclusion was ordained, inevitable.

Louise said, "I've noticed comfortable men are often bachelors. I know another one just like you. I suppose you get used to spoiling yourselves and don't want to give anything up."

A glass was put down somewhere. "You look very nice today," Corder said.

"I've just had a bath. I used some new perfume . . . here, smell. . . ."

Footsteps crossed. Another glass was put down.

Louise sighed, harshly. The sounds of their movements went on for several seconds. Then Louise sighed again, this time with pleasurable surprise.

"You certainly *don't* need any stimulation," she whispered.

And Corder murmured huskily, "I've been thinking about it all morning."

"That's more than obvious." Then she cried out. "Please! Don't be so impatient. These are my best tights! Wait a minute. . . ." Her shoes clattered on the floor and there was a sound of zippers and fabric rustling.

When she spoke again there was laughter in her voice. "Men always undress so quickly. . . . You turn away for a moment and then when you turn back there it is."

Then she was gasping, struggling. . . .

It stopped abruptly as Denis pressed the hold switch. He was frozen there, his eyes closed. He went back to pour another whisky, measuring the tot against the light. He didn't hear the ambulance that burst suddenly through the square with its bell ringing. As it faded he went back to the tape deck.

When he pressed the play button again there was only the soft frictional sound of their bodies moving together, which went on and on. Denis sat down and let the whisky lie sacramentally in his mouth again before swallowing.

Louise began to moan softly and springs creaked as their bodies shifted. "Please, darling . . ."

Corder didn't answer. Only the springs went on creaking.

"Darling, that hurts. . . ." Then her sharp intake of breath, which was repeated again and again.

Corder growled in his throat and there was silence

suddenly except for their quickened breathing. Louise cried, "What's wrong!"

"I just don't want to come yet! Don't move . . . don't move or you'll wreck everything."

Denis turned his head slowly to stare at the running tape. He was conscious suddenly of holding his own breath, afraid that if he, too, moved, the spell would be broken.

Then Louise said tearfully, "Please . . ." and this time the animated rhythm of their bodies made the chaise drum lightly on the floor.

Corder said "Jesus" once, in tones of anguish, and Denis closed his eyes, waiting.

As usual her call started quietly, winding up like a siren, and it seemed to hang for an age, pulsating and melancholy, before dying in her throat. The sound of their exhausted breathing filled the room.

Denis sat on for nearly five minutes while the tumult died and knew that something was different. With Corder there had come a change . . . she treated him differently from the others. Not with respect, it wasn't that, but with Corder she seemed to lack the authority she'd formerly had over the rest. He sat there troubled, pressing his moustache with a finger.

Then Corder whispered something which he didn't catch, and Louise said, clear-voiced, "He's earned his reward."

But there was no sound of movement—only her breathing had changed, becoming erratic. Corder sighed deeply.

Denis drained his glass suddenly. He was an *écouteur* who had become expert at his occupation, he knew each variation in the decibels of intercourse. Every sound had its familiar subtlety so that he could tell at once the difference between the oral kiss and the genital kiss, as he was also able to visualize exactly the relationship of their bodies. He had even developed an intuitive flair, so that like a chess player moving a piece, he could frequently anticipate the response of their bodies from one position to the next.

Corder's breath was urgent, sobbing, and he had begun to moan, a confusion of pain and ecstasy that ended in a cry. Again Denis waited for calmness to return. Meanwhile, he knew by the whisper of clothes that Louise was dressing again.

She said with amusement, "Now I'll have to have *another* bath."

Then, after almost two minutes of silence, Corder said, "What time is it?"

"Twenty past three."

Corder's bare feet thudded on the floor, first one and then the other. "I don't know if I'm strong enough to get dressed. . . ."

"I'll make a nice cup of tea."

"Christ, how wonderfully British. . . . How *super!*" Corder's shoes were on; Denis had heard the faint squeak of their soles.

"Come and talk to me in the kitchen while I make it."

"Okay."

Louise's footsteps went away and a door opened. Corder began to whistle tunelessly while he finished dressing, then after a minute his footsteps followed hers. Denis went over and punched the speed button. Only the Westminster chimes marked the passing hours. There were no more voices. Denis stood there frowning. There was something else that was different with Corder. The others had always talked there, in the room, and none of them had been offered tea that he could remember.

The tape flapped and he snapped off the player. Then he put the reel in a carton and labeled it carefully. "Corder, 12 Nov." He locked it away in the cabinet with the others.

As the Peugeot swept up the drive past the cottage, Denis could see a light in the living room and the blue flicker of the television. Corder was somewhere out of sight in a chair. Denis drove on, scattering the fallen leaves, and circled the forecourt. As he waited for the garage doors to open he saw that Louise was still in the kitchen, sprinkling something into a saucepan.

After he left the garage he went hurriedly around to the front door. He hung up his jacket and document case and was putting on his cardigan when she came through.

After she'd kissed his cheek she said, "I'm cooking a super supper . . . a sort of pilaf."

She moved on to open the door of the living room. Denis said, "I'm not hungry . . . not yet."

The tone of his voice stopped her and she turned back, watching him. "Are you not, then," she said quaintly. She leaned against the wall, one hand spread behind her.

Denis moistened his lips. He said in a voice that wasn't quite steady, "Let's go upstairs."

She watched him with clear, speculative eyes, and put her other hand to the wall to join the first. "My, I believe we are quite excited."

Denis smiled back at her. "Yes, we are . . . quite."

She pushed herself away from the wall and walked close past him to go into the kitchen. After a moment he heard the click of switches on the stove. Then she came back again, smiling faintly, and started to go slowly upstairs.

Denis followed her, his eyes fixed on the swing of her hips.

The vole was dead.

Corder found it not far from the house, near some old quarry stones that had been set in the grass. It was lying on its side, dewdrops on its fur. Corder had come out to sniff the morning as he always did, making one circuit of the house and orchard before going inside to work. This morning there was a touch of frost, and the smoke from the fire he'd lit in the living room was going up in a straight column. He crouched on his haunches and took the vole gently into his hand. As he turned it over he saw that the skin was unmarked. There were no wounds, its heart had just stopped beating in a moment of helpless terror.

Corder knew that the cat had killed it in play. Any other of the vole's natural predators, the little owl, a hunting fox, a heron . . . they would all have eaten it. (There was a heronry on the marsh below Framlingham Castle, not five miles away, which he had visited during his first week.)

He imagined the cat carrying it to the center of the lawn, releasing it, watching its hopeless terrified run with sulfur-yellow eyes. While he stood there with the body cold and wet in his hand, the Peugeot came lunging down the drive and swung away toward the lane. He saw Fleming give his usual careless wave, but he didn't wave back. He walked slowly up to the cottage, stroking the vole gently at the nape of its neck, as if it were still alive. It had wandered too far. Nature always killed off the most inquisitive, and the most trustful. Trust was a false weapon, like a boomerang, that came back and chopped your own head off.

He got an old newspaper from under the stairs and put it under the vole on the round table; then he opened his portfolio and got out his drawings. He knew that rigor mortis would have passed by midday; the little body would be fully relaxed, and he'd be able to check the accuracy of his work.

He turned it over on the paper to dry the other side.

[2]

Denis had made his usual morning round of the show-room and the workshop. There was a truck off the road with a rear wheel bearing gone, and he'd had to reschedule some of the repair and maintenance work. So it was ten o'clock before he settled at his desk. He drew his document case toward him, unlocked it, and took out the house mail. Each morning he picked up the mail from the doormat at home and brought his own to the office. He saw the tape lying there as he locked the case again and was aware of the uneasiness he'd felt the day before. As he flipped through the mail he saw that he'd brought one of Louise's letters by mistake.

It was from the bank, he noticed as he turned it over. He laid it aside and opened his own letters and the office mail, which contained a check from Mrs. Ferris for the alarm installation. After he'd sorted and filed it all, he picked up Louise's letter again. It was her half-yearly statement, probably. His finger went automatically to push at the bristle of his moustache. In his mind he already knew he would open it, just because it was there. He had not, after all, taken it deliberately. All the same, he delayed a full minute more before tearing the envelope.

The current account was on top. He glanced down at the regular credits (from his own account) and her weekly withdrawals. Then he lifted the page to see her savings account and was suddenly motionless. There was a balance but only in the amount of about twenty-five pounds. Sixteen hundred pounds had been withdrawn a week ago.

Denis was aware that his heart was beating faster than usual, and he covered it with a hand as though this might slow it down. He dropped the statement back on his pad and started to move around the desk uncertainly. A week ago would have made it about five weeks after the arrival of Corder, he thought, relating it unconsciously to yesterday's uneasiness.

He came back again, grinding a fist into his palm, and sat down. Why, his mind was saying, why? But it could not voice the thought that terrified him most.

Corder buried the vole in the late afternoon before going up to the woods with his gun. He used the coal shovel and dug a hole not far from where he'd paunched the hare and buried its guts. And then as an afterthought he walked through the tangle of mint stems and picked up the urn that was lying there on its side. He carried it back to place it on top of the newly turned earth. The wild flowers were all gone, but there was still some yarrow showing in the long grass. He picked a couple of stems and dropped them in the urn, smiling as he did so.

Today he loaded the shotgun as he moved through the orchard. If he got sight of the cat it would get a load of buckshot, right up the jack.

Louise called Denis early in the afternoon.

It was Wednesday, the day she washed the hair of the old people who lived in the almshouse at Framlingham. Denis listened to her voice carefully as she spoke, listening for straws in the wind, straws to make bricks, bricks that would build God knew what.

"I'll be a bit late," Louise said. "Joyce Manning wants me to go back to the farm afterward. She's giving us some apples . . . and some William pears."

"That's all right, darling. I don't mind."

"I've fixed us an easy supper . . . we can eat as soon as I get in." There was a short silence, then she added, "Are you very busy?"

"So-so. I may go home early and rake up some leaves."

Another silence. Though neither of them had anything to say, neither wanted to be the first to ring off. Louise said, "Don't put them on the rose bed, let Mr. Wilson deal with them."

Last year Denis had tipped them among the roses and the first gale had blown them all over the lawn again. He turned in his chair and reached across to open the door noisily. "Oh, dear," he said, "I'm afraid I'm wanted. See you later, darling."

"Bye-bye."

He hung up and leaned across to close the door again. Then he sat back, staring at the phone.

At four o'clock he put a plain envelope in the typewriter and addressed it to Louise. Then he slipped her bank statement into it, sealed it, and dropped it in a side pocket. After that he looked up the Mannings' telephone number in the book and dialed it.

When Joyce Manning answered he said, "It's Denis. Is Louise with you?"

"No. Is she coming?"

Denis hesitated. "Well . . . I thought she said she was."

"She's not here yet . . . when she called she just said she'd try and make it. I've got some apples for you."

"That's very kind of you. Bob well?"

"Mmmmm. He's always well."

"We must meet and have a meal together soon. Goodbye, Joyce."

"Just a moment. . . ."

"Yes?"

"What did you want?" Joyce said. "Am I to give Louise a message?"

"Well, it isn't important," Denis said carefully. "I was just going to tell her to call at the pub on the way home. I may walk down there."

"I'll tell her if she comes. Goodbye, Denis."

"Bye." He hung up.

Standing there beside the desk he ran his finger lightly to and fro across his moustache. He realized that it had been foolish to call too soon because he still didn't know whether she would go there or not. He picked up his document case and went out slowly.

On the way to the car he crossed tne square to post the letter to Louise. Then he drove home, faster than usual. Louise wasn't there. After he'd changed into his cardigan he walked around the house looking at familiar things. He could not have said what he was looking for, only that he would know if he found it. Or, by some paradox, if he didn't find it. After walking the ground-floor rooms he went upstairs.

He stood for a while on the landing, looking down at the cottage. Corder must be there, he thought, because a thin skein of smoke was rising from the chimney and a shirt was flapping lazily on a clothesline in the orchard. Denis went on to the upstairs bathroom and washed his hands. He looked in the two spare bedrooms, pushing open the sliding doors of the long wardrobes which Louise had insisted on. Children's clothes would have hung there. Denis shivered. The heating was turned off in these two rooms except when they had guests. He went through to the master bedroom, closing the doors carefully.

Louise's dressing table was in the usual disarray, with powder scattered on the glass and lipsticks standing in groups like batteries of tiny missiles. Denis leaned forward into the triptych mirror, which he often did when he was alone, to see the sides of his head as others saw it.

When he walked into the closet and turned on the light he had a sense of foreboding. It was almost a dressing room, bounded on one side by the width of the huge Tudor chimney. A hanging rail with all their clothes ran half the length of it. Beyond were things like their luggage, a linen chest, and a dressmaker's dummy Louise had bought soon after their marriage. As Denis stood there in the doorway he knew that things were not as usual, and a moment later he realized what it was. Louise's furs were missing

119

from the far end. He walked slowly down to the empty hangers. When they married, Louise had owned a rather old-fashioned but valuable Russian sable; then on their tenth wedding anniversary he had given her a silver mink.

He put out a hand that shook slightly to grasp the rail by the empty hangers, and his other hand went automatically to his moustache. In a voice that quavered slightly, he said, "Please God. . . ."

Then he was hurrying away through the bedroom to the landing where there was a small mahogany wardrobe. He snapped open the doors, but they weren't there and he went back to the bedroom. Feverishly he opened and slammed the drawers of the big chest. Then, shaking his head, he walked into the closet again, and went down it flipping hangers to make sure they were nowhere there. They weren't. He snatched up suitcases, opening them one by one and dropping them.

The furs were packed neatly in a monogramed suitcase, second from the bottom. Wedged beside them was her jewel case. Louise wasn't given to wearing jewelry, but she had inherited several valuable pieces from her grandmother. The contents of the case, he realized, together with the money that had been in her savings account, represented all her worldly possessions. Denis stayed on his knees, knowing with certainty now that she was planning to leave him.

He closed his eyes and felt the onset of oppression again, as if unseen hands were clasping his head, as if the blow had been physical.

Something else had startled the pheasant, far out in the sugar-beet field, and Corder had shot it cleanly as it came by him in a long glide. He'd been out for an hour or more.

When he got back to the house he went straight in to lay it on the newspaper where the vole had lain. Then he went out to the orchard again to get his shirt, which was still damp. He hung it on a hanger in the chimney corner to finish off.

He was just going to put the kettle on for coffee when he saw Denis Fleming coming up the path.

He opened the door and said, "Mr. Fleming."

"Good afternoon, Mr. Corder."

"Please come in . . . I was just going to make some coffee."

"Not for me," Denis said primly. He waited near the door, looking uncertain. "You're quite comfortable then. . . ."

"It's great, Mr. Fleming. Exactly what I wanted." Corder went over and put a log on the fire.

"Getting on with your painting?"

"Yes, getting on fine. And I've had some good shooting too. Hardly had to buy any meat yet. Why don't you sit down?"

"Kind of you." Denis sat on the edge of the settee. He was staring up at Corder, silhouetted against the window. He was imagining Corder naked, the way Louise saw him He didn't speak. He was afraid that if he spoke, whatever he said would be related to his secret fear, and Corder might be warned. He wanted Corder to betray himself.

And then, as if the thought had been audible, Corder said, "I'm going away."

Denis waited. "Back to London?" he said casually.

"Christ, no. I don't mean *right* away. I'm taking the Land-Rover up to Norfolk for the weekend."

Denis pressed his hands together, stared down at them. He remembered that a couple of weeks ago Louise had told him she was planning a weekend in London, which she usually did two or three times a year. So it was possible that she was leaving him *this* weekend. But why had Corder told him . . . there hadn't been any need.

"I want to see the Nature Conservancy place. . . . I called them up, and they were most helpful. One of the wardens is going to show me around on Saturday afternoon. Then Sunday I'm doing the Castle Museum in Norwich, where they have one of the finest natural history collections in the country."

Denis said, "I've never been there." He covered his mouth briefly. "I suppose that's a terrible admission, really. I've been to Framlingham Castle . . . that's where Mary Tudor was living when she was called to the throne."

"Is that so." Corder moved the new log with his toe, nearer to the center of the fire.

Denis stood. "I'd better go back. Louise'll be home soon." He was looking down at the pheasant; the white ring around its neck was almost perfectly symmetrical. He put a hand down instinctively, to stroke the glossy plumage.

He said, "Pretty things . . . aren't they." He wanted to leave but felt rooted there against his will.

"Take it if you'd like it, Mr. Fleming. I've got another hanging in the cellar."

"No thanks." Denis shook his head. "I don't like killing things . . . unless it's absolutely necessary." Denis wished he could stop talking and go away. He was doing what he'd been afraid of doing . . . talking about his secret fear. "After all," he said, "they haven't done anything wrong. . . ."

"They wouldn't know, would they?" Corder said. "They haven't got a conscience."

"*We* have a conscience," said Denis in his prim voice. "*We* know."

Corder looked away at the barrel clock on the mantelpiece. It was six o'clock. He silently cursed Fleming because he'd missed the weather forecast on television. He was a man who lived with weather forecasts.

With his hand on the rust-colored breast feathers, Denis said, "Louise's hair used to be this color . . . she dyes it now."

Corder didn't know what to answer so he stayed silent. With relief he saw Denis start moving toward the door. "Well, I must get back. She'll be home soon."

"Drop in any time, Mr. Fleming," Corder said. "Always pleased to see a friendly face."

"That's kind of you. Have a good weekend."

Denis walked out to the driveway through the misty air. He could hear pheasants coming in to roost higher up in the woods. Their calls sounded like football rattles in the stillness. As he closed the wicket gate he saw Corder wave from the window. He waved back.

Walking on, he was visited by a grotesque, irrational thought . . . that he wouldn't mind, really, being shot by Corder. He imagined the alignment of the barrel with Corder's huge bulk behind it. . . . Corder's great muscles bunched and tense, and then the roar and the searing flash . . . the hot gush of blood. The image had gone in a moment. It had been no more than a flicker on the retina of his psyche.

Since she'd left the village, Louise had been driving with her parking lights. As she came up past the cottage, in case Corder was watching, she flicked the headlights on and off.

She caught her breath as Denis showed suddenly on the edge of the beam.

She slowed down and stopped beside him. "Hello, darling . . . I thought it was you."

Denis opened the door and climbed in. The sweet smell of apples was mixed with her perfume. She said, "I stopped at the pub just in case."

"I didn't go down after all. I've . . . I've been talking to Corder."

"How is he?" Louise was accelerating up the rise. She flicked the headlights on again and left them on.

"He seems very comfortable. He . . . he shot a pheasant today."

"Good for Mr. Corder." The headlights came toward their own pale reflection on the garage doors, which opened up. Louise drove in and pulled out the pistol-grip handbrake.

In the darkness Denis said, "Shall I take in the apples?"

"No. We'll store them here. Do it tomorrow."

They had supper in the kitchen and afterward watched television together, an old movie with Robert Mitchum, who reminded Louise of Corder. Denis sat in a wing chair slightly out of Louise's view.

Denis's head was aching, and the glare of the set hurt his eyes. He sat with an elbow on the chair arm and his forefinger pressing hard on his upper lip. He roused himself with a start as Louise said, "Too boring. To think we used to wear those dreadful clothes. Do you mind if I turn it off?"

"Please do."

"I'm going to go to bed and read. Why don't you do the same. . . ."

"I shan't be long." Denis yawned. "I'll be up in about half an hour."

"Mind you do."

She left the set and stood over him. "You're looking tired." She bent and kissed the top of his head. "In case I'm asleep."

As she opened the door he said idly, "By the way . . . it's this weekend you're going to London, isn't it?"

"*This* weekend?"

"I thought you said. . . ."

"No, darling, it *was* to be this weekend but I told you yesterday that Norma had phoned to say it wasn't suitable. So I'm going in two weeks. Don't you remember?"

"I can't have been listening," he said feebly.

Then Louise said, in a voice full of amusement, "You're not *planning* anything, are you, darling? If I thought you were going to be unfaithful I wouldn't go!"

Denis still had his headache when he awoke, and he went into the bathroom and took paracetamol before plugging in his electric shaver. Returning from his shower he found the bedroom empty and he knew that Louise must be getting his breakfast in her bathrobe. He went into the closet for a tie and stopped dead. The furs had been taken from the suitcase and were back on the hangers again.

Whatever plans had been made had obviously been changed. He remembered her words: "It *was* to be this weekend . . . but Norma said it wasn't suitable."

When he went down to the kitchen, his bacon and eggs were on the table, and Louise came from behind the stove to hang an arm loosely around his neck. "I'm tired," she said wearily, "but I've done my duty. I'm going back to bed for an hour."

Later, driving to the office, Denis decided that it could have been that she wasn't quite ready to leave him yet. Perhaps there were other assets to be realized or perhaps there might be trial weekends to put him off guard. He blinked painfully as he drove. The one thing he'd always feared was going to happen, and the irony of it was that it was the one thing against which he had hoped Corder would protect him. He moved against the safety harness, straining it, and groaned out loud.

The tenant of Burdock Cottage was a concept designed to save them from scandal. Local lovers, like Colonel Ferris, must sooner or later cause comment, give rise to gossip, or even worse. But with Louise's lover living in, so to speak, they were relatively secure. There was nothing to be seen.

Waiting at an intersection, Denis closed his eyes again. He murmured, "Oh God. . . ."

Life without her would be unbearable, he thought, driving on again. There was no one else. No one else would ever understand. Only Louise. He could never give her up, and so, logically, there was only one way out of the wood. The line of pain across his head was as tangible as a hard-pressing hat brim as he turned into the yard and backed the Peugeot into its place. He got out and walked slowly with his case, exhausted by the anxieties of the night. When he got to the shop, he stood for a long time staring in at the turning wall spit. There were so many considerations . . . because he had a conscience and Corder had a conscience, and Corder couldn't be killed like a pheasant, not without knowing why.

The broilers and kabobs turned slowly in the simulated glare, but what Denis was seeing was the body of Corder, its fat and muscle dissolving slowly in the blazing heat.

"Are you all right, Mr. Fleming?"

His head snapped around. Rosemary had opened the shop door and was looking at him curiously. He was aware that his hands were clenched.

"Yes . . . yes, I'm all right. Just thinking."

"Oh, yes." She closed the door and was going back to the counter again before he followed.

"I was thinking about changing the display," he said.

She smiled, with embarrassment. "Sorry I disturbed you. You . . . were looking rather . . . well, stiff. Like the man who had the fit that day."

"I've a bit of a cold," Denis said. "Have you taken the mail up?"

"It's on your desk, Mr. Fleming."

He read the mail with only half his mind. There was nothing of importance. After a while he took a work pad from a drawer and started to make rough sketches of the interior of the cottage. Then from the filing cabinet he took the technical data of the alarm system he had installed for Colonel Ferris. All morning he made drawings and modifications, and later he brought up the spare alarm system from the stock room and checked it over.

Most days he lunched in the back bar of the Bull Hotel with Tony Knott, an antique dealer on Church Street, but today he drove to Ipswich and spent an hour in the reference room of the borough library, checking several volumes on chemistry to find the expansion rate and other characteristics of hydrocarbon gases. Back in the office he worked on through the afternoon, planning circuits. What made it all so complicated, he admitted to himself, was not only that fastidious part of him which could not kill in cold blood, but also that, having killed, there must not be any aftermath. Nothing must remain that could haunt him, let alone incriminate him, in years to come.

He went down to the stock room again about mid-afternoon and came up with an intercom layout. He checked it through, marking off each component against a diagram. When the staff went home, he was packing the system away again. He realized his headache had gone, and some of his anxiety had gone with it. As he stood at the mirror combing his hair, he was surprised to see he was smiling unconsciously. He decided to call Corder *now* . . . tonight.

Corder had shot a brace of pigeons just as it was getting dark. He had promised them to the landlady down at the pub. Now he sat by the fire with the gun dismantled around him, drying off the parts and pulling the barrel through with a brush. As he lightly oiled the extractors and started to assemble the thing, the phone rang.

"Corder? Is that Corder?"

At first Corder didn't recognize Fleming's voice. It sounded lighter and somehow more cheerful than he remembered. "What can I do for you, Mr. Fleming?"

"I just wondered . . . I hope you won't think I've got an awful cheek . . . but when you're in Norwich would you mind if I did a bit of wiring in the cottage? I never really got everything done before you moved in."

"Don't worry on my account, Mr. Fleming. Everything's great as far as I'm concerned."

"It'll have to be done sometime." Denis sounded irritated. "I thought it was rather a good opportunity."

"Okay. Suits me. I'll leave the key in the usual place, shall I?"

"No, that doesn't matter, I have a key of my own."

"That's fine, then, Mr. Fleming. Make some coffee if you feel like it."

"I will," said Denis, almost gaily. "And I hope you have a most enjoyable weekend in Norfolk. It's very beautiful."

"Thank you, Mr. Fleming. Goodbye."

"Cheerio."

Denis hung up and pushed the phone to the back of the desk. He was smiling still, and after a moment he started laughing. It was the gleeful laughter of a small boy, and it seemed to take hold of him gradually, until his whole body was shaking with it. His head dropped to the blotter and rolled helplessly on his hands. The paroxysm was a long time passing and finally gave way to intermittent sobs, and when he raised his head he saw that his hands were wet. They were tears, he realized, and they surprised him as much as the smile had surprised him earlier.

"A fully automated death," he said clearly. *"Fully* automated." He repeated it with emphasis, as if it was a very important point, as if he was selling death to some customer, there in the room with him.

[3]

Corder went up to the house on Thursday after lunch. Louise, he noticed, was angry about something, and they made love more vigorously than usual, ending up on the floor. Afterward Corder lingered on, drinking another whisky. He wouldn't have admitted it to himself, but it wasn't purely sexual therapy that brought him up to the house once or twice a week. He also had a need to talk to someone.

Louise hadn't dressed but had gone upstairs carrying her clothes. Corder walked around while he waited for her. He put his glass down on the player cabinet and noticed idly that it was quite warm. He spread his hand on it for a moment. Then he saw Louise back in the hall wearing a white toweling robe.

She said, "Here a minute," and crooked a finger. And when he joined her she added, "If you're not in a hurry, bring your drink upstairs and talk to me while I have a bath."

"Okay."

When he got upstairs she was lying in the scented water with her eyes closed and her hair tied up with a man's tie. Corder sat on the toilet seat watching her.

He said, "What's wrong with you today?"

"Nothing's wrong today that isn't wrong every day." Her eyes didn't open. "Life is a bloody muddle, that's all."

"You seem to have it worked out."

"That's what everyone thinks about everyone else's problems."

Although Corder was conscious of the need to talk to her, he certainly didn't want to hear about any problems. That was the start of getting involved, the beginning of the end. He stood up and moved about uneasily. After a moment he tried weighing himself on the bathroom scales.

"Don't break them," she said. "What time are you leaving? I mean for Norfolk. . . ."

"Oh, around lunchtime tomorrow. Old Bessie won't do more than forty miles an hour, and I want to get settled in a pub before dark."

"When are you coming back?"

"Sunday evening or Monday morning." Corder went to look out the window. From the higher elevation he could see down through the trees to the cottage. His blankets were on the line, airing in the weak sunlight.

Behind him the water lapped as she moved her legs, and Corder said, "Your husband's going to do some work in the cottage while I'm away."

"What kind of work?"

"Oh, some wiring job."

She was silent again until he turned around. Then she said, "What wiring job?" Her voice was casual.

"He didn't say. Something he meant to do before."

She stood up then and flipped out the plug, and he passed her a long towel. She said, "How very nice of him." She was frowning.

Corder was afraid that she was going to start on her problems again. "It's time I was getting back," he said quickly. "I've left a stew cooking."

Louise dried her legs and stepped into Moroccan sandals. She walked into the bedroom with the towel draped around her. "All right," she said in a faraway voice.

"What shall I do with my glass. . . ."

"Leave it."

"Here?"

"Anywhere you like."

She was annoyed, and he knew it was the start of a situation where he should take her tenderly by the shoulders and she would tell him all about it. He put his glass down resolutely on the chest of drawers and said, "Well, goodbye. . . ." Then to take the edge off he added, "By the way . . . do you have a cat? I often hear a cat yowling up in the woods."

She was standing in front of the mirror, hugging herself in the towel. "No, we haven't got a cat."

"Well, maybe it's a wild one," he said as he went out.

He'd gone down the first flight and was turning on the landing when she came out of the bedroom after him and leaned on the banister rail above. "We haven't got a cat," she said in a voice that was unnaturally loud. "Neither do we have a little puppy dog. In fact we don't have a fucking thing like that. Instead we have a lodger in the cottage."

Corder was conscious of hidden danger. There seemed nothing to say, so he just blew her a kiss and went on down the stairs and out of the house. As he went, the phone started ringing in the hall. Walking down through the rough grass to the creek he remembered the warmth of the record player where his hand had rested. She must have been playing records before he arrived, he thought absently.

On Friday morning when Denis got up he saw that the glass of water and the sleeping tablets were on her bedside table again, so he went quietly downstairs and got his own breakfast. But he'd forgotten a handkerchief, and he had to go up before he left the house. This time Louise's eyes were open and she looked at him drowsily. "Darling. . . ."

"I'm all right, darling . . . forgot a hanky, that's all. I'm just off."

"Darling?" She half sat up.

"It's all right," he said reassuringly.

Then in a completely clear voice she said, "What are you wearing?"

He was wearing his old cord trousers and a jacket. "I'm taking the day off. I thought I'd look in at the office this morning and then finish off the wiring at the cottage over the weekend. Mr. Corder's going to Norfolk."

"For how long?"

"Just the weekend. He said he didn't mind."

134

"But I thought you'd done all that."

"I did the new wiring, but I never renewed the old. And it's really a fire hazard. If the insurance company ever inspected it we wouldn't get coverage."

Louise lay back and closed her eyes, and he went to the handkerchief drawer. Returning, he stopped by the bed again. "I'll be on my merry way," he said and, bending, lightly kissed her forehead.

She opened her eyes. "You're very jolly today, darling. . . ."

"Am I? I expect it's the prospect of having a couple of days off. I'll be home for lunch." He closed the door when he left and ran lightly down the stairs.

At the office he went briefly through the mail and then had Barney up for half an hour to discuss the schedule of work. He told Barney that he'd look in again in the morning and if anything dramatic cropped up they were to call him at home or at the cottage where he'd be working. He arranged for Padley, one of the apprentices, to come out and help him that afternoon.

Then, while Padley carried the equipment out to the Peugeot and loaded it, Denis went to the stock room. He took a couple of detonators from a box left over from the time when they'd laid cable to the Woodbridge yacht marina and had to blast a channel. He packed them carefully in an old transistor carton.

It was half-past eleven when he parked outside Sam Doe's. Sam was the agent for the bottled-gas company and Denis had a thirty-two-pound drum loaded into the Peugeot.

"I'll have to charge you the deposit on the drum," Sam said. "Why do you need it, anyway?"

"I may be having the driveway resealed, and once they start I don't want any traffic until it's set." Normally Sam delivered the drums in an old Albion truck.

Denis got home again soon after twelve to find Corder had already gone, so he parked the car close to the wicket gate where the Land-Rover usually stood. He walked up the grassy bank and through the buddleia screen to the house. As he let himself in through the french window he could hear Louise laughing and he realized she was at the telephone in the hall.

On the tail of the laugh she said breathlessly, "You shouldn't *say* things like that ... *please....*"

Denis stood there thinking that Corder must be calling from some pub up the road, somewhere where he'd stopped for lunch. Then Louise said, "Fifteen days? I hadn't counted ... it sounds like eternity...."

Denis turned back to the window, hesitating. Then he reached out a hand and opened it again. When he slammed it noisily there was immediate silence from the hall. Then she said hurriedly, "Thank you so much. Goodbye."

When she came to stand in the doorway Denis said, "Hello, darling."

"Darling," she echoed mechanically. "I didn't hear the car...."

"I left it down at the cottage. I've got some gear in it."

"Lunch is in the oven, we can eat when you like."

"I'd like it now."

"Super."

She went back into the kitchen. Denis waited for a moment, his mind busy. Fifteen days of eternity took them to the weekend after next. The weekend Louise was going away.

When he went down to the cottage after lunch, Padley was already there, eating sandwiches. Denis set him to work laying PVC cable around the ground floor while he worked upstairs. He took up floorboards and opened the trapdoor into the roof space. Both the alarm system and the intercom only needed small-gauge wire, which was easy to handle, and by the end of the afternoon the circuits were nearly complete.

They stopped to make tea about four o'clock and while they were drinking it Padley said, "Shouldn't think you'd get many burglars out this way, Mr. Fleming."

"No," said Denis carefully. "But it gives people a sense of security to know they have it, don't you think?"

"Maybe it does. I can come over tomorrow and help you finish off if you like?" The workshop staff didn't work Saturdays.

"Oh no," Denis said.

"What about the plastering?"

"There isn't a lot, and I've got some ready-mix plaster." They had channeled out the walls and buried the cable where necessary.

Padley went home at five and afterward Denis got a spade from the garage and started cutting another channel across the lawn, carefully laying the turf aside. He worked on in the half-light, trenching across the rose bed and up to the garage wall, which he drilled at ground level. Then he threaded the cables through heavy-duty conduit pipe and laid it from the house to the garage. He raked the earth back again, replaced the turf and the paving slab where it crossed the path, and tidied up. The sky was fading as he finished.

After he'd put the spade in the garage, he went back to

the house and turned on the lights. There were cartons and reels scattered all over the floor, and he sorted out some intercom panels and started to connect them up. There was a moving coil speaker and a carbon microphone in each panel, and since he was wiring it on a party system there'd be no need for multiple cable or push buttons. In an hour and a half he'd connected them all up and left them hanging, ready to fix to the walls after dinner.

He drove the Peugeot up to the house and put it away. They had a drink first and then ate supper in the kitchen. Louise had made a pie with some of Joyce Manning's apples. As he was eating it she said, "Shall I come down with you?"

"I shouldn't." Denis's headache had come back again, a thin, hot wire tied around his head. "It's not worth lighting the fire, and it's a bit on the chilly side."

"How is he keeping things. . . . I suppose it's a frightful mess."

"No, it's quite tidy. He hasn't used the teapot. I think he uses a saucepan to make coffee."

When he left she had stacked the dishes in the dishwasher and was looking at television. She said, "Please don't be late, darling," and she leaned forward out of the wing chair so that she could see his face. "I haven't spoken to a soul all day, you know."

"I won't be more than an hour."

He took the flashlight but the sky was deep and bright and he didn't need it. Pipistrelle bats fluttered up and down the driveway above his head, feeding on the insects between the trees. When he turned to look back at his own house, he saw that Louise was standing in the french window staring out.

He stopped in the dark, looking back at her. Suddenly his body was twisting with hatred, and his face was contorted like a gargoyle's. He pushed out his tongue, forcing it as far as it would go.

Corder arrived home on Sunday afternoon around four. The wind was in the northeast, bending the crack willows beside the pond and tearing away the last of the leaves. After he'd lifted out his duffel bag he buttoned down the canvas back of the Land-Rover. It was cold inside the house, and yet he'd been living there long enough to have a feeling of coming home. He lit the oil stove, plugged in the electric heater in the bedroom, turned on all the jets of the gas stove. Then he started a fire with some dried sticks of elder, and as it got going he made a pyramid of logs, clean white ash, which he'd sawed himself in the first week. On the edge of the fire he noticed pieces of carton that hadn't been burned and the ends of some electric cable.

He filled the kettle and put it on to make coffee, and while he was standing there in the kitchen he heard Fleming say, "Good evening, Mr. Corder. Did you have a nice weekend?"

He looked up, expecting to see Fleming in the doorway, thinking that he hadn't heard him come in. But Fleming wasn't there. He walked back to the living room, puzzled.

"Fleming?" he called. "Where are you?"

"Everywhere. The voice of conscience come to haunt you."

This time Corder was aware of the distortion, and the voice was coming from near the door. He moved over, searching, then he saw the intercom panel screwed to a timber. "Okay," he said, close to it. "You can come out now."

Waiting, he heard footsteps and then a door shut. He moved to the fire, expecting Fleming to come down the staircase, and at the same time feeling annoyed that Fleming had been hiding in the house when he arrived. But there was no sound from upstairs, and Corder was wondering what the hell was going on when there was a knock at the front door. He opened it. Fleming was facing him, panting.

"Good evening. Sorry if I startled you."

"That's okay. Come in." And as Fleming went ahead of him Corder said with a slight edge to his voice, "What the hell is all *this* about. . . . I thought you were just doing a few repairs."

"Well, I've done those too." Denis turned. "I'm . . . I'm sorry if I upset you."

The words were said without conviction, and although Corder didn't know him very well, he was aware of a change in Fleming's manner. He was kind of cocky and excited today. Corder said drily, "What's the point of it?"

"You can communicate with every room."

"Who do I communicate with. . . . I can talk to myself without intercom."

Denis moved away. There was a new board on the easel, unmarked. "I haven't only put in an intercom," he said. "There's something else as well."

Corder heard the kettle start to whistle in the kitchen. He said, "Excuse me," and went through and snapped off the gas. While he made the coffee he called, "I haven't noticed anything. What is it?"

Fleming appeared in the doorway. "A burglar alarm," he said.

Corder laughed in spite of himself. "You're kidding."

"No. I'm quite serious."

Corder put the coffee on a tray with milk and two mugs. Fleming moved ahead of him back to the living room. Corder said, "Why a burglar alarm! For Christ's sake . . . who do you expect to break in here?"

"Nobody . . . really."

"Then why waste the money?"

Denis moved away to the west window to look up at the orchard. The cloud ceiling was low, there was no sunset tonight. He said, "If you want to know, I had the stuff in stock down at the shop. So I thought I'd use it up on the cottage."

Corder poured his coffee and said, "Would you like some?"

"No thanks."

Corder took his coffee to the fire, which was just catching enough to give some heat. "Why give yourself the trouble?" Corder shook his head slowly and for the first time felt uneasy. "I don't get it . . . what's going on. . . ."

Without turning, Denis said pedantically, "You're quite right not to believe me. I was afraid you wouldn't."

"Well, what's going *on!*"

Denis turned. "You'll have to promise me not to tell anyone. Louise . . . my wife mustn't know."

"Okay, I promise."

Denis let his breath go. He smiled. "May I sit down?"

"Please do."

He sat and looked up at Corder. "You see, it's all to be a surprise for . . . for Louise. When you give up the cottage in the spring, I'm going to bring Louise's

141

parents down from Scotland. They're both getting on now, and the old girl's crippled with arthritis and can't move around much. You see, with a simple intercom system like this she'll hardly have to move around at all. She'll be able to talk to the old boy wherever he is, and it'll also save them a lot of stair climbing. What do you think?"

"Well, I guess that anything that makes life easier is a good thing."

"I even wired in the garage . . . that's where I was speaking from. And I thought while I was doing it I might as well put in a burglar alarm at the same time. You know how nervous old people are. I want to make it as easy and comfortable as possible . . . for Louise's sake, then they won't be bothering her all the time to do this and that."

Corder went to switch on a table lamp and pour himself another cup of coffee. In the sudden light he noticed Fleming's forehead was shiny with sweat.

Denis blinked. He felt half happy, half anxious. "I . . . I'll go in a moment."

"That's okay, Mr. Fleming."

Denis moved out of the light and nearer the fire where Corder had been standing. "It's just that I think you should know how the alarm works. Actually it's terribly ingenious."

"All right . . . tell me about it."

"I'll have to show you," Denis said. Then he must have become aware of the sweat on his face because he took out his handkerchief and wiped it vigorously. "If we can go upstairs. . . ."

He went first, turning on lights, and Corder followed curiously. On the upstairs landing Denis said, rather formally, "May I go into your bedroom?"

"Surely."

He went in, switching on the light. Corder waited in the doorway. Under the china plaque with its border of roses Corder saw another intercom panel.

Fleming was looking excited and boyish. He said, "Come and stand beside me." And as Corder went to stand there awkwardly, he moved away to the head of the bed. "All the doors and windows have contact switches, you see, so that the moment anyone fiddles with them the alarm goes off. You set it here, last thing as you get into bed, or you can set it by a switch in the garage. . . ."

"The *garage*. . . ."

"Well, if someone broke in when you weren't at home it would still scare them off. But what's really clever is that even if a burglar *did* get in, he'd still be detected." Denis pressed the switch down with his foot. "Pretend you're a burglar . . . start moving around."

Corder shrugged and walked out onto the landing. Immediately a strident ringing started from somewhere downstairs. Corder froze and the ringing stopped as Fleming kicked the switch.

He said, "That resets it again."

"Well, what did I do?" Corder said.

"There's a trembler switch under the floor . . . it needs forty pounds to set it off, so a dog or a cat couldn't activate it."

"Well, thanks for showing me."

"I haven't finished. Now try going downstairs."

Corder went on lightly down the staircase and again the bell started. It stopped as Fleming kicked the switch again and walkea out onto the landing above Corder. He said, "That was a photoelectric device. There are three on the stairs . . . and you'd never find them. What you did then was to interrupt the infrared beam. Now try downstairs. . . ."

Corder said, "Do I have to? I'm prepared to take your word for it . . . no burglar can move an inch."

There was a short silence. "As you wish, of course," said Fleming. He came down the stairs after Corder, who went to pick up his coffee. "Please just look at this last one, it's one of the only ones visible." Fleming was standing by the front door. Corder went to stand beside him.

Denis pointed to a newly cut recess on top of the door where a spring clip on the frame was holding a short stud screwed to the door. "You see," he said, "the door holds it in the closed position, but if you open it that starts the alarm." He opened the door, and Corder saw the jaws of the clip separate. "The points are silver-plated to avoid corrosion," Denis said. "Of course it's switched off now."

Corder went back to the fire. With finality in his voice he said, "Well, thanks for showing me, Mr. Fleming. I don't think I'll bother switching it on for myself, but it looks very efficient."

Fleming came halfway toward him and stamped a foot suddenly. "Actually the whole of this floor is sensitive. You couldn't move an inch without setting it off." He turned away. "I'm sorry I've taken up so much of your time, Corder. It was awfully decent of you to listen." He opened the door. "Cheerio."

"Good night, Mr. Fleming."

He watched Fleming go around the side of the house by the orchard and set off across the rough ground. "Poor little bugger," he said out loud, and pulled down the lamp above the easel.

Denis had come to the ditch and jumped it, and as he

went up the rise on the other side, he leaped suddenly into the misty air, punching out with his fist. It had gone better than he had expected, and he was in a state of ecstasy. He punched the air again and again, like a soccer player who had just scored a marvelous goal.

[4]

Sitting at his desk during the next ten days, he tried to be calm. Patience was a virtue of the hunter, a virtue that Corder must possess.

Also like a hunter, he had watched for further signs of Louise leaving him, but there had been few enough and they were mostly ambiguous. Once he'd discovered her sorting records into "his" and "her" piles, because it took her so long to go through them, she explained. His headaches had come back and were almost constant now so that he had to dose himself with paracetamol two or three times a day.

Since Corder had come back from Norfolk there had only been two tapes to file away in the cabinet. Both occasions had been somehow muted, as though they were also waiting. Louise was going to London tomorrow in the evening, but he still didn't know when Corder would follow, except that it wouldn't be right away because that would be too obvious. And besides, that morning when he'd passed Corder in the drive Corder had given him a roll of film to leave at the pharmacy. Denis wished he knew, but the matter had not been discussed in those moments of languor that followed the lovemaking. If they *had* been discussed it must have been when they went to the kitchen for tea or back to Corder's cottage. They were meeting today, he knew, because the arrangement had been made a few days before at the end of the last tape. Denis held his head, feeling a sudden increase in the pain.

He heard the tinkle of the tea tray outside his door, and a moment later Rosemary came in and put it down on his desk. "Oh, thanks," he said casually. He waited until she'd gone before he got two cookies from the tin and poured the tea. He sipped it and noticed it was not as hot as usual. No doubt they had been larking about downstairs, he thought, as they sometimes did during the morning and afternoon breaks. And his pot had been left to stand and grow cold.

He was hardly conscious of the surge of anger that suddenly bore him to the door out of control, and almost before he knew it he had stumbled down the first flight of stairs and was leaning over the banister, shouting.

"Where's that girl . . . where is she! Tell her I want her back here! Immediately!" He was aware of the pale face of an apprentice staring up at him.

Then Barney walked calmly into view beneath him.

"What's wrong, Mr. Fleming?"

"Tell that bitch I want to see her now!"

Barney didn't answer. He just turned quietly on his heel and went into the shop. Denis went blindly back to his office and stood by the desk. His hands were shaking. The staff was taking advantage of him the way everybody else took advantage of him. They were patronizing him the way the customers patronized him, like that arrogant bastard Ferris. In spite of his rage he saw clearly that it was his fault . . . that he had let people make him what he was. He was too bloody amiable.

He heard tapping at the door and said, "Come in."

The door opened and Rosemary said, "What's wrong, Mr. Fleming?"

"The tea isn't hot."

"Oh, I'm sorry. I'll make some fresh."

When he looked around she smiled at him in the faintly silly way she had. He felt another spasm rising uncontrollably and he drew his hand back slowly. Then it came slashing down and he felt pain as the cup went spinning, to crash against the wall. The fragmentation seemed to take ages, the pieces turning over and over in the air. Tea dripped down the wall. Denis stood there for a long time blinking at it.

When he turned around she'd taken the tray and gone. The door was open, and he went across to close it before sitting down at his desk again. Two flights of Phantoms shot over the town suddenly and the room shook. It was as if heaven was echoing his rage.

There were tear streaks down her temple, Corder noticed when he turned his head. He said gently, "What's wrong?"

She turned her face quickly away from him. They were

lying on the carpet, still naked. He put an arm around her smooth waist and drew her close against him. "What's wrong . . ."

"I . . . I don't know. I'm just feeling low today."

Corder was silent. He hadn't wanted to visit her today either, but they'd arranged it and he'd thought she might be disappointed. He realized now that she hadn't really desired him either. It was an inevitable step in their relationship that neither should want the guilt of being the first to cry halt. Half an hour ago while she was squirming on top of him he thought he'd seen the faintest expression of disdain in her eyes. The familiarity of love bred its own kind of contempt. He began to ease away from her, afraid of her silence.

"When are you leaving?" He had started pulling on his clothes.

"Not till after dinner. I get to London about nine thirty."

She sat up suddenly and leaned back on her hands, and he was relieved to see she was smiling. "Mind you men behave while I'm away," she said.

"I can't answer for your husband." He stepped into his cord trousers and zipped them up. Louise was watching him, still smiling. "What's funny," he said.

"Nothing," she drawled. "I'm feeling better, that's all."

"Not low any more?"

"Not low any more."

One of her hands came up to press a breast lightly. "You hurt me today. You don't realize how strong you are sometimes."

"I'm sorry. I guess I was carried away."

"I don't like being hurt."

Corder went over to the sideboard and poured water

into his empty whisky glass. He drank it off, filled it again, and carried the second glass back to the chaise. Louise was pushing her arms through the straps of her brassiere and hooking it.

Corder said, "I've been meaning to ask you . . . why didn't you ever tell me more about the other tenant?"

"What other tenant?"

"The one who had the cottage during the summer."

"Oh, him. I thought I *had* told you." She started to dress, moving quickly.

He reached up a hand to clasp her wrist lightly. "Tell me about him now."

"He was a bore. He also thought that coming here was a sort of quid pro quo, so he stopped paying his rent . . . as if I was so unattractive that I had to pay for my pleasure. Then finally he had the nerve to go and order a suit of clothes in Ipswich and have the bill sent to me."

"What happened?"

"Oh, we had a frightful row, and he just disappeared."

"I was working on the theory that he was buried in the herb bed. I found a little funeral stone there."

She looked at him calmly. "If *I'd* buried him anywhere it would have been in the rose bed. Blood is very good for roses. You may not know it, but that is why some hospitals have very fine roses." Corder laughed and she added, "Someone said he went to Australia." She snapped the waistband of her tights and bent to pick up her dress "That thing you found was about all he left behind."

"You must admit it was a funny thing to leave. . . ."

"Not really. It was for his cat."

"Oh, I get it. His cat died."

"No, his cat *didn't* die. He used to feed his cat out of it."

"You're joking."

"No, I'm quite serious. You see, he was a stonemason and he worked at the funeral shop in Woodbridge. That was one that went wrong . . . maybe he put the wrong date or something like that."

Corder remembered, wryly, all his night thoughts, all the Gothic theories he'd constructed. When he looked up, Louise was feeling her ear, shaking her dress.

"I've lost an earring. Stand up a minute. . . ." While Corder stood, she moved the cushions and pushed her hands down the sides of the chaise. "Damn! They're my favorite pair."

Corder got down on his hands and knees and started to search the floor. He worked steadily across to the wall behind the chaise and then down toward the record player. He was sweeping a hand under the record player when suddenly he glanced up. "What's this?" His voice was troubled.

"What's what?"

Corder leaned further under. The plastic case of the microphone was taped to the underside of the player. Corder said, "It looks like . . ." He put up his hand at the same time and felt warmth again. He was still suddenly.

"Darling, what's wrong? Darling. . . ?"

Corder withdrew quietly and swung to face her. "What *is* it?" she said in sudden fright.

He shook his head quickly and grabbed her arm, moving her toward the door.

"You're hurting me . . . please . . "

As he pushed her out of the door and followed, closing it, she swung to face him. "For God's sake, *tell* me. . . ."

Corder said, "There's a microphone taped under the record player and the cabinet's warm . . . somehow he's fitted a tape recorder inside it." And as she shook her head stupidly he went on, "Don't you *see?* It's Denis! He knows about us. He's . . . he's collecting evidence."

Louise stayed against the wall, her mouth half open, watching him. "God knows how long it's been going on," he said. He turned away suddenly, leaving her, and went back into the room and over to the player. He followed the cord that ran a couple of yards along the wall to a socket. Bending, he pulled out the plug.

He turned. "It's okay," he called. "I've unplugged it." And he went back into the middle of the room, waiting for her. When she still didn't come, he returned to the door. He took her arm gently. "It's all right," he said and drew her into the room.

"We'll have to do something, though," he said. "God knows how long it's been going on. Is there a screwdriver anywhere?"

"Behind the clock. He keeps one there."

Corder turned the clock slightly and found it. He started to undo the screws at the back of the cabinet. The tape deck was vertical with the spool half run, and the meter read 640. Corder studied the controls for a moment and then plugged it in again. As the tape started he punched the rapid rewind and watched the meter spinning back. When it was nearly to zero he stopped it.

He looked up to where she stood watching in silence. He said, "Now don't say anything. I'm running it through again." He pushed the recording button and the rapid-forward button and sat back on his heels while the spool hummed. He stopped it around the six hundred and twenty mark. Then he said, "I'm starting it again now. Wait in the garden . . . we can talk there." He watched her turn mechanically and go down to the french window.

After she'd opened it and stepped out, he pressed the

recording button. As he bent to screw back the panel he saw the electric clock screwed to the top of the cabinet, which must have been the way it was switched on. He fitted the screws, one by one, as quietly as possible and put the screwdriver back behind the clock. He stepped outside himself, closing the french window gently.

She was standing by the corner of the house, quite still, with her back to him, and he realized that apart from telling him where the screwdriver was she hadn't spoken a word since the moment he'd found the microphone.

He went down to her and said, "I've cleaned the tape and rerun it. Christ, what a *mess*. . . ." He walked around to face her. "How did he *suspect!*"

"I don't know," she whispered.

"And more important, what's he going to do? Has he ever mentioned a divorce?"

"No, never. It's . . . it's never been discussed."

Corder walked around again in a small frustrated circle. "What are we going to do?"

Louise shook her head. "Just wait, I suppose."

Corder took her forearm and held it. "Listen," he said, "one thing you can do is look through the house, in his desk and places. Maybe you can find the other tapes he's made. He must keep them somewhere."

"I'll look, but what if I *can't* find them. . . ."

"Well, we can't do anything about it. Except we'd better go easy for a bit . . . not see each other."

She sank against him with her eyes closed, and Corder found himself holding her with real concern. It was as if the danger that was going to divide them now, could have been something, paradoxically, that might have held them together. Then Louise left him suddenly and hurried away around the side of the house. Corder took a pace after her and hesitated. Instead he turned off and went down the bank, making for the rear of the cottage. The afternoon was cooler but still bright, and somewhere on the other side of the wood he could hear mallard passing and the flat, repetitive call of the female.

He stopped when he reached the stream, and in a moment of blinding clarity he suddenly knew why Fleming had wired the cottage and put intercoms in every room. He intended to use a tape recorder there to spy on Corder as he did up at the house. Corder decided to make a thorough search.

Denis wasn't sure how long Barney had been there. He had heard him put the tray down, of course, and go on over to the window. And now Barney's silhouette had the outline of a rainbow against the brightness of the sky. He was also aware that Barney had been speaking to him, but his voice had been an echo only, as empty as the silhouette.

Until now, when Barney said, "You're not listening, Mr. Fleming."

Denis cleared his throat. "I'm sorry, Barney . . . I was thinking about something else. Tell me again. . . ."

"It's just this, Mr. Fleming. Nobody is indispensable. We can run the place like clockwork, and the accounts won't matter for a couple of weeks. You need a break . . . it can't go on this way." Barney moved slightly across the window and the spectrum of color went with him. "I had to spend an hour talking young Harrison around last week after you'd stirred him up. He wanted to clear off and join one of the rental mobs in Ipswich. . . . You really need to get away from it for a bit, Mr. Fleming."

Denis said, "I'm sorry." He saw the tray beside him and poured fresh tea automatically.

155

As he raised the cup to his lips Barney said, "Well, what about it?"

"I *have* been under a bit of a strain lately," Denis said carefully. "I hope you'll explain to Rosemary. . . ."

Barney said with an edge to his voice, "Will you take a few days off?"

Denis looked up, blinking, and noticed that the rainbow around Barney's silhouette had gone. Suddenly he realized that the distortion had not been caused by the sky behind but by the moisture in his own eyes. He wiped them briefly and looked away, embarrassed.

He said, "All right. I'll take next week off."

And as if sensing his advantage, Barney said, "From tomorrow." His voice was firm.

"I wasn't coming in tomorrow anyway. I've . . . I've got something on at home."

Barney came away from the window at last. With his hand on the door he said, "Don't get me wrong, Mr. Fleming. We like it here, and we want to help you. The Robin Hood principle works both ways."

Denis nodded. He heard the door close behind Barney. He had wanted to tell Barney about Corder, about the fully automated death he'd arranged for Corder. It was very appropriate, really, for someone who came from such a technological nation, a nation which had been able to send men to the moon and back. He shut his eyes again because the light was hurting.

Corder had been up and down the house looking in every cupboard, behind every curtain, even in the cellar. But there was no sign of a tape recorder anywhere. Then he remembered the garage and went out to look there. On the wall by the workbench he saw the new intercom panel and on the bench itself was a litter of wire clippings Fleming had left behind. Corder crawled all through the old sagging furniture and delved in the dusty trunks and even the piano. There was nothing there. He went back to the house to wash.

While he was in the bathroom he heard Fleming's car swish by and accelerate away up to the big house. He went downstairs, kicked up the fire, and lay down on the settee, frowning. He remembered the first time Fleming had called. Fleming had practically asked him to go up to the house, he'd implied his wife was lonely . . . had even suggested that he, Corder, might like to paint her. He wondered what the bloody hell Fleming was up to! Maybe Fleming was involved with another woman and was setting up to ditch his wife.

Corder stood up heavily again and moved past the easel to stand in the window. There was another highly colored sunset, all reds and mauves, like the illustration of a particularly nasty operation in some medical textbook.

As Denis circled the drive he saw that Louise's Renault was already parked at the front door. When either of them went to London, they always took a car to the station at Woodbridge and left it there. It meant there was no fuss about getting back. Denis put his own car away and carried his document case into the house. He hung it in the hall and shed his jacket as usual.

Louise called to him from the living room. "I'm in here, darling."

He went in. "Darling."

They kissed with slightly more warmth than normal, and Louise said fondly, "I'm all packed up and supper's on. I thought then we'd have time for a little drinkies."

157

"I'll miss you." Denis walked on to the cabinet to pour himself a glass of malt whisky. He turned, holding it up before he drank it. "Bon voyage."

Louise smiled and toasted him back. "Mind you eat properly. . . . I've left lots of things. Mr. Corder gave me half a hare last week and I've made a terrine. It's in the larder. And there's lots of steak and frozen vegetables on top of the freezer. And anyway you know Norma's number if you want anything . . . she'll take a message if I'm out."

"Don't worry. I'll be all right." He had no headache at the moment, but he was conscious of his heartbeat. He walked over to the chaise and sat across it. "When do you think you'll come back?"

"Oh, sometime on Wednesday afternoon. I'll be home in time to do dinner."

Denis closed his eyes. "I've had a rather hectic week. I may take a few days off. . . . Barney can manage. We might go to Norwich one day when you get back."

"Yes, we could do that," she said.

When he opened his eyes again there was a refraction of colored light around Louise's head, giving the appearance of a halo. He wiped his eyes again with finger and thumb.

Then Louise said, "I don't know that Mr. Corder is terribly happy down there . . . from something he said the other day."

"Why not?"

"Oh, I don't know. Maybe he finds it a bit lonely."

Denis stood up and walked the room in silence. As he came back to pick up his glass he said, "It's such a business finding another suitable tenant. Are you sure you're not mistaken?"

"It's . . . well, it's just a feeling I get. I may be wrong."

"It would be a bit of a blow." Denis went to pour himself another drink.

Behind him he heard Louise stir, and a moment later she went past him. "I'd better look in the oven."

After supper she went up to her room to get ready, and Denis stacked the dishes in the dishwasher and started it up. Then he went through to his desk in the dining room. He got the local paper from his document case and opened it to read. Among the classified advertisements for services he found his own, which read:

FLEMING'S FOR TELEVISION AND ALL
ELECTRICAL INSTALLATIONS,
41 MARKET HILL, WOODBRIDGE

He had a long-running contract with the paper, and every Friday he checked that it was inserted and that the spelling was correct. He turned back to the center pages and went on reading odd items of local news until he heard Louise come downstairs. When he went out to the hall she was wearing her sheepskin and her zip-up knee boots.

They went out into the dark together and embraced beside the car.

"Take care of yourself, darling."

"And you," he said. "I'm sorry you're going." He didn't know why he said that; the words had arrived in his mouth unbidden.

"But you wanted me to go. You said it was good for both of us. You . . ."

"Of course, don't worry, darling."

Louise got into the car and pushed open the window. "I'll call you tomorrow evening."

"Not too early . . . I may go down to the pub."

She twiddled a gloved hand, the headlights leaped to life and the car moved off, with the cold engine missing slightly. He waited, watching the lights as they swept the edges of the drive until they finally disappeared into the lane. He went back into the house and straight through to the living room. Getting the screwdriver from behind the clock, he undid the back of the player cabinet and punched the rewind button. When he ran it forward again, there was only silence until just after halfway, when the West-minster chimes rattled off four o'clock.

Denis stayed motionless on his knees. He knew that someone had cleaned the tape and reset it at four.

Corder knew.

Up in the bedroom he laid out the thick sweater and his old cord trousers, getting everything ready for the morn-ing. Then he found a BEA flight bag left over from some holiday and took it downstairs to pack. Methodically he laid out everything he was going to need on the kitchen table. Shockproof flashlight, transistor radio, the detona-tors. Then he settled at the table to cut sandwiches, filling them with thick slices of the terrine. As well as the sand-wiches he got an apple pie from the freezer and a dozen or so of Joyce Manning's eating apples, which he put in a plastic bag. He packed all the food in the flight bag, and at the last moment he went up to the bathroom for a bot-tle of paracetamol tablets in case his headaches came back. He stood there double-checking in his mind everything that he needed.

Afterward he went back to the living room and poured himself another whisky. He sipped it standing by the french window and looking down at the lights of the cottage. He wondered what Corder was doing.

A moment later he had set down his glass and stepped out into the night. He walked carefully around the flower beds, keeping inside and parallel to the driveway. There was no moon but the sky was luminous, and when he came to the screen of buddleia he groped his way through it with no difficulty. After five minutes he had worked his way to the top of the bank in front of the cottage.

The driveway was white below him and the windows of Corder's living room a bright square of orange beyond. He could smell the scented woodsmoke from Corder's fire. There was no sign of Corder, but he could see a reflected glow in the orchard which must be coming from the kitchen light.

Then behind him in the woods somewhere he heard the plaintive howl of a stray cat. After a moment it sounded again, a little closer. Denis crept down the bank to a clump of dogwood beside the drive.

He saw Corder suddenly come from the kitchen back to the living room and stand motionless in the window.

Corder had been washing the day's dishes when he first heard the cat. Just as he finished and was going back to the other room he heard it again. It was hunting, somewhere near the orchard, he decided. He waited by the fire, listening, then he crossed to the wall where the gun was hanging and lifted it down. He broke it and dropped in a couple of cartridges before opening the door and stepping out into the night.

He stood a full minute, his eyes growing accustomed to the dark. An owl called in the distance. It wasn't the little owl, but the screech of a barn owl on the wing.

Denis was crouched with his breath held. He had seen the light gleam on the gun barrel as Corder stepped out, and now he could just see Corder's silhouette as he turned his head to stare up at the lights of the house. With a dry mouth Denis watched the gun barrel swing as Corder turned. In spite of the tension which gripped him, he thought fancifully for the moment of the night before Agincourt or some other medieval battle, when armed men stared across the darkness at the lights of each other's encampments.

Then Corder moved off out of sight around the side of the house. Denis withdrew slowly and went up the bank on his hands and knees, keeping low. When he reached the buddleia screen, he straightened and walked on through the rose beds toward the french window.

Corder awoke later than usual, about seven thirty. That was the time on his alarm clock and he had just started to yawn when Fleming said, in a voice that shook slightly, "Good morning, Corder . . . I've come to kill you. For God's sake don't move off the bed."

Corder's head turned, but Fleming wasn't in the room. "Oh, Christ," he said irritably. Then his eye caught the intercom panel, and he could just hear the faint rasp of Fleming's breathing.

Fleming said, "It's not a joke, Corder. I know all about you and Louise."

Corder shook his head. "What the bloody hell are you playing at?" he shouted. Then he flung off the covers and stood up.

"*Don't!* Don't move, Corder, or you'll kill yourself. It's not a joke! Please believe me."

Then Fleming sobbed twice and whispered something Corder couldn't hear. Corder looked around uneasily.

"For God's sake, don't move!" Fleming's voice was

agonized, desperate. "If you move you'll only precipitate events. You see, if you set off the burglar alarm you'll blow the whole place sky-high."

Corder sat on the edge of the bed and looked slowly around the room, at the threshold where he'd set the alarm bell ringing the other day, at the landing beyond. He ought to walk out and down the stairs laughing, but there was something crazy about Fleming's voice.

He stood up again, gingerly, facing the intercom. Trying to keep his voice calm and good-humored he said, "All right . . . I'm frightened to death, Fleming. Now what do you really want. . . ."

Fleming didn't answer; there was only the sound of his unsteady breathing. After a quarter minute, Corder said again, but with less confidence, "Okay. I tell you I'm scared to death. Now what is it?"

"I'm going to kill you. I'm sorry, Corder . . . there's no other way . . . I've spent nights thinking about it."

Then Fleming began to cry, a long, wavering sound that made Corder shiver.

PART
IV

[1]

Corder sat hunched on the bed telling himself that he must keep calm. Also that he must try and keep Fleming calm. Of course, he realized now, Fleming was a nut. It was something he should have realized before. The whole idea of the tape recorder was a bit nutty, and fixing up the intercom and so on. He also remembered things that Fleming had said, like the semimystical conversation they'd had about shooting.

The room was almost fully light from a watery sun just above the horizon. "Bloody hell!" he thought wildly.

Then from the intercom Fleming began to speak hurriedly in a low voice, like a priest gabbling a prayer. "Do you know anything about hydrocarbon gases, Corder? They have a relatively low expansion rate, lower than gelignite, in fact, but they have a fantastic destructive power. It's like muzzle velocity . . . the lower it is, the more penetration you get. I'm talking about when the gas is mixed with air, of course. The butane in your cellar is a hydrocarbon gas, but you probably know that."

Fleming's voice faded slightly and then came back more strongly, as if he was moving around, doing something else while he talked. "There's just over forty cubic meters of air in your cellar, which mixed with between one and two drums of gas will give a maximum effect. In fact there's enough of the mixture to blow up a whole row of houses. I went down to the cellar and rolled them over and opened the taps long before you woke. It's heavier than air, you know, so it can't get away. I also wired a detonator in place of the bell in the burglar-alarm system."

Corder's head snapped around suddenly. "You're crazy, Fleming. You've had your little game . . . now switch the bloody thing off!" In the silence that followed, Corder cursed himself for the outburst. On no account must he get rattled.

"You'll probably smell the gas when you get out on the landing."

There was a long pause before the pedantic voice went on. "That is *if* you get out on the landing. And I want you to be quite certain, Corder, that any interference with the wiring would be suicidal. If you break the circuit by cutting a wire, or interrupt the span of an infrared beam, a relay is released and the firing circuit is complete."

"Where are you, Fleming?"

"In the garage, of course. Out of harm's way." Corder heard his faint, tinny laugh.

Corder slowly transferred his body weight to his feet, pressing them against the boards. The under-floor switches operated at a pressure of forty pounds, Fleming had said. But they had been standing by the bed with the circuit live and nothing had happened until the moment he'd stepped through the door to the landing. Corder stared at the floorboards there, but they told him nothing. It wasn't possible to tell which one of them had been taken up. Corder stood slowly, and for the first time he thought he smelled the faint sourness of the gas. He put out a foot and was annoyed that it shivered slightly. He walked two more paces along the line they'd been on the other day. From there he could see through the window down to the garage.

He watched for several silent minutes, but he couldn't see Fleming clearly. Just once he thought he saw a shape move behind the glass of the window. He took two steps back the way he had come and bent suddenly to flick the switch on the mopboard.

"It's no good, Corder," said Fleming clearly. "It's unserviceable now. I wired it out."

Corder leaned a hand against the wall between the intercom panel and the plaque which said "Bless This House." He wiped his forehead briefly across his pajamaed arm.

"Bloody hell," he thought again wildly.

Denis was standing by the window with the field glasses raised. He had seen Corder step slowly into sight to look down at the garage and then step back again. He'd waved, but obviously Corder couldn't see him. He lowered the glasses and set them back on the workbench. The flight bag was unpacked, and he ate a sandwich while his eyes roamed across the rubbish, looking for a chair. The springs were bursting from both the padded chairs, but beyond, on the wall, a deck chair with faded striped canvas was hanging. He lifted some apple boxes out of the way and a set of golf clubs with cane handles, until he could reach it.

All the time he was conscious of Corder's steady voice.

"I wasn't going to see her again, Fleming . . . I give you my word on that. Even before I discovered the tape, I'd made up my mind. It's all over. And it didn't mean much anyway. You can ask her, Fleming, she'll tell you it's true. It wasn't a grand affair . . . something casual that happened. You can't kill a man for that reason, Fleming."

Denis opened the frame with difficulty and set the chair up by the bench. In the fold of the canvas a small black spider was hiding in a cocoon of silk. As he lifted it tenderly away, it fell and fled across the floor. He started dusting down the canvas with his hand, still oblivious of the voice from the speaker.

"Don't you see that you can't kill a man for what I've done . . . it isn't rational. You've brooded about it, Fleming, and you're not seeing it in its true perspective. If you think about it calmly for a moment, you'll see that what you're doing isn't logical. And another thing you should remember is that I'm only partly to blame . . . it's not all *my* fault."

Denis lowered himself into the chair experimentally and raised his feet to the bench. He closed his eyes.

"Fleming! Are you there! Can you hear me!"

Denis opened his eyes but didn't answer. As Corder suddenly went on, he closed them again, clenching them against the Lilliputian shouting.

"You're not solving anything with this bloody madness! I haven't been the only one . . . there've been others. And if you kill *me* you won't stop it. There'll be somebody else. You'll have killed me for nothing! Think about it, Fleming. . . . Think what you're doing!"

But Denis didn't hear, he had his hands pressed against his ears. When he took them away after a minute, the shouting had stopped. There was just the tick of Corder's alarm clock and, faintly, the sound of Corder's breathing. He stood up and picked up the field glasses again.

As he trained them on the window, Corder said, "They'll hang you or whatever they do here, you realize that, Fleming."

"Not any more. There's no capital punishment now."

"Then they'll put you away. You won't be able to keep her then."

Denis moved nearer the intercom. "They won't put me anywhere, Corder, because after the explosion there won't be a shred of evidence. Can't you see that? Believe me, I've spent a great deal of time planning the whole thing in such a way as to ensure there'll be nothing to give me away. It will have the appearance of a straightforward accident, for which the insurance company will recompense me."

He put out his tongue at the intercom set, slowly pushing it as far as it would go.

Corder was conscious of his body being damp, conscious of the mechanism of fear.

"I'll just stay here, Fleming. I won't move. . . . Somebody'll come in the end."

"And open the door?" Then Denis added, "You'll be killing an innocent person as well."

"Oh, Christ . . . " Corder whispered to himself. Only slightly louder he said, "They'll lock you up anyway because you're insane!" Then in spite of himself he was shouting again. "Because you're a bloody maniac! Do you hear that, Fleming?"

There was a click, and the sound of a screaming pop group filled the room. The words were unidentifiable, it was just a tribal roar of strings and voices. Corder sat down on the bed, gripping his thighs with his hands. It was no good, he realized, trying to talk Fleming around. Fleming's crazy world was impregnable. Fleming had made up his mind. Corder looked out across the landing again. If he could get there he knew he was safe, because he'd stood there the other day. And if he could find a way of avoiding the stairs. . . .

He stood up slowly again, considering it. If he could build a bridge through the doorway he'd miss the first switch. His head turned slowly as he searched the room. He said "Floorboards," to himself, and flipped back the small rug. The boards were old and black, and in places the gaps were almost half an inch. He looked around for a lever. Then he thought of the bed frame. He ripped off the covers and the mattress and then, very gently, the old-fashioned mesh on its wood expander. Beneath that he saw with relief there were angle irons slotted into the head and foot pieces. He turned the frame gently on its side and tried to loosen one of them with the heel of his hand, but they were too tight.

His shooting brogues were at the head of the bed and he put them on his bare feet and laced them up. It took him two minutes to kick one of the angle irons loose. He leaned the ends of the bed gently against the wall and took his brogues off again; then he took the angle iron and worked a corner of it into a gap between the floorboards. There was a crack as the timber split, but it made a bigger gap into which he could push the end.

When he levered the next time, the whole board came up slowly, pivoting on an edge and bringing the nails with it. He took out three boards in quick succession. He was beginning to work with confidence because he'd suddenly thought of a way to beat Fleming. He'd go out through the ceiling and push a hole through the roof tiles and get down the outside, then across the lean-to at the back if he could.

It wasn't possible to smash a hole through the lath and plaster in the bedroom, and the likelihood was that if he tried he might set off one of the vibrator switches. But above the landing there was a trapdoor made for the purpose. What he needed now was a buttress out there on the landing to support the other end of his bridge. He looked across at the chest of drawers. It was four yards away, against the west wall. He looked at the floor, wondering whether to chance it. Then suddenly he realized he didn't have to. He could lever up the boards all the way to it. Then if there was a pressure switch underneath one of them he'd see it. He worked steadily, taking out seven more boards. There was no switch, just a junction box for the electricity. He walked carefully along one of the cross joints, took out the drawers one by one, and emptied out his clothes. Then he carried the drawers back and stacked them in the middle of the room.

As he turned away to pick up a plank, the music stopped as suddenly as it had begun.

Corder waited through a long silence, until Denis

said, "What are you doing, Corder?" Then after a pause, "You wouldn't be so foolish as to start a fire. You'd be gone long before the fire brigade got here."

Corder continued to wait with the plank resting lightly against his shoulder. He waited because he was conscious that there were two possibilities of salvation. One was that he could get out himself with all the attendant risks, the other was that he could slowly gain some authority over Fleming's sick mind. For the first time since the nightmare had started, he was conscious of an advantage. Fleming wanted to talk to him, wanted to communicate, wanted to explain. While he waited quietly, Fleming's frustration seemed almost tangible.

Then Fleming spoke again, this time close and loud. "Whatever you're up to, Corder, I don't want you to die under a misapprehension. I . . . I want you to know why."

"Because I have a conscience?" Corder said with irony. "Is that what you mean?"

"I'm not killing you, Corder. I've only provided the means. In the actual event you'll kill yourself."

"The distinction escapes me. You could say I've never killed a pheasant. I haven't physically done it, the gun has done it for me."

There was a pause before the music started again with a blare.

Corder picked up the plank, hooked it into a drawer, and raised it. He stood with his eyes closed for a moment, not praying but mustering a will to act in the face of known danger. He had to do it, he told himself, and logic was on his side. If there was a switch somewhere in the doorway, it seemed improbable that there would also be one on the landing just beyond. He swung the plank slowly, his muscles braced, until the drawer was opposite the doorway; then he eased forward slowly, maneuvering the drawer through. He froze once as it scraped on one side, but then it was clear.

He pushed it out slowly, taking more strain, until the drawer was halfway across the landing and near the banister rails; then he lowered it inch by inch until it was resting on the floor. He withdrew the plank back into the room with him.

What sounded like a very bad hotel orchestra was playing music from "The Merry Widow."

[2]

Denis was eating a sandwich in quick little bites, and when he'd finished it he licked each fingertip precisely.

There was a trunk open behind his chair, with old Christmas decorations hanging over the edge of it. He hadn't found anything of interest in it. He took up the field glasses again but Corder wasn't visible. Perhaps he was already on the landing. . . . Denis had seen the plank waving around and had guessed what Corder was up to. He lowered a hand to turn off the music. Then he listened with his ear close to the intercom, but there was no sound.

He wanted Corder to speak. He wanted to provoke Corder.

He said suddenly, "I knew about the others, Corder," and waited. "Corder?"

"Then why pick on me?"

"That's what I want you to understand . . . it's not just because you're my wife's lover that I have to . . . to dispose of you."

"Why don't you say 'kill me,' Fleming?"

Denis closed his eyes, and his hand came up to press his moustache lightly.

"Say it, Fleming! You're going to *kill* me!" Corder's voice repeated it as if he knew he was pressing on a nerve. "You'd better turn up the music again."

Denis's hand lowered to the transistor and hesitated. Then he pushed it away and moved nearer the intercom. "I tell you I *did* know about the others, Corder. Rob Walker, Ferris, the dentist . . . but I understand all about it. She . . . she could never have children, you see. Did you know that? So it's a sort of compensation, I suppose. I've tried to understand it that way."

"Then why pick on *me?*"

Denis closed his eyes again, patiently, wanting Corder to understand. "Because you're the first one she's wanted to go away with."

"You're talking balls. It's never been in her mind."

"I know better. With everyone else . . . I shared her. But you wanted to take her away. Each time . . . each time there was someone new I used to wonder if it would be someone who'd want to take her away from me . . . or someone she'd want to go away with. But it never was and gradually I came to realize I was safe, that going away

178

wasn't what she wanted, that I had a marriage of sorts after all."

"I tell you that you're wrong. We never even discussed going away. You can *ask* her."

"But I can't. She's in London. And you see, it really isn't necessary, because I have proof that she was leaving me."

Then Corder was shouting again, rattling the diaphragm of the speaker. "The reason she's leaving you is that she knows about the tape recorder, Fleming. She knows you've been spying on her."

Denis clicked on the radio again and spun the thumb wheel to maximum volume. He said, "Poor Corder," but it was drowned by an electric organ belting out some terrible medley of old tunes.

Corder's hands were shaking as he turned over a drawer and set it on the floor at his feet, a couple of paces from the doorway. Then he gently laid two planks on top of the two drawers, and he had a bridge across the threshold. There was a tear down one leg of his pajamas, and blood had dried there from where he'd scratched himself on a nail. He put one knee up on the bridge and was still again, summoning the will to act.

Then he put both hands forward on the plank and drew up his second knee so that all his weight was on that part of the floor where the drawers rested. Very slowly he started crawling, his eyes fixed on the planks as they began to sag under his weight.

The music stopped again suddenly, and the creak of the boards was audible. Corder went steadily on. He was pouring with sweat, which made the cloth of his pajamas feel like slime.

He was conscious of the doorpost going by, then the railings of the landing, then he was nearly to the drawer. Just as he reached it, Fleming called his name. "Corder!" It echoed around him, coming from the speakers downstairs as well. He stayed huddled at the end of the planks, breathing deeply.

"You've got it all wrong, you know, Corder."

Corder, unhearing, carefully drew his knees under him and got up on one of them. Then he stood slowly, feeling with his hands for the ceiling and catching the frame of the trapdoor. After steadying himself, he pressed a palm against the flap. It was stiff and didn't move. He started tapping around the edge of it with a closed fist.

Then, as if he could see him, Fleming said clearly, "By the way . . . I should warn you about the trapdoor to the roof space. There's a contact switch beside the catch, if you look carefully you'll see where I had to recess the frame. In fact it's quite hopeless to think of getting out and I shouldn't even try if I were you. Even if you get as far as the landing, you can't move an inch on the ground floor."

Corder sank back slowly to his knees. He put one hand on the banister rail and lay half across it and half across the planks. He stayed still, breathing deeply. Where his head touched his forearm the sweat started to make slug trails through the dust.

"Corder, why don't you answer me?" Fleming's voice had become reasonable and kindly. "Listen to me . . . I assure you that you've got it all wrong. Louise has known about the tape recorder for two years!"

Corder raised his head slowly. "That's balls too."

Although he'd only whispered, Fleming must have heard, because he said, "It's not balls, Corder. Why do you think she only made love to you in my living room? She never made love to you here . . . or in her bedroom, or in the woods. Why, Corder? Think about it a moment."

Corder raised his head slightly and rested his chin on the rail. He was feeling colder, and he realized suddenly that Fleming must have turned off the oil heater. He would have to have done that, or there would have been a premature explosion. "Come up to the house in five minutes," Louise had said, that first time. But there was really no reason why they couldn't have had it off then and there in the cottage. And always afterward, as Fleming said, it had been on the chaise longue . . . next to the tape recorder. Then again he remembered that she had always taken him out of the living room to talk. In the kitchen once . . . and the last time in the bathroom when she'd talked about life being a muddle. He knew then with a kind of fatal certainty that Fleming was speaking the truth. That bitch, he thought. That *bitch*. . . .

She had been in on it all the time, was in on it now, even! Maybe she had guessed what might happen to him.

Fleming was speaking again in his voice of sweet reasonableness, as if he was the one that was sane and Corder was off his head. "She never really thought about the tape recorder . . . that would have made her self-conscious. We never discussed it, either. You see, you were part of a ritual, Corder, a game even, and now you've spoiled it for all of us. You were having pleasant dalliance on your doorstep, so to speak, without any great inconvenience, Louise had some sort of substitute for the children she can't have, and I had my marriage of sorts. You spoiled the game, you spoiled the whole thing."

Corder began to laugh softly. It grew louder until the boards trembled under him. It turned suddenly to rage.

"Why don't you be *honest,* Fleming," he shouted. "You didn't only have a marriage of sorts going, you also had a nice little perversion going." His voice rose, almost out of control. "Why don't you admit it, Fleming! Why don't you admit that you're a *dirty, stinking pervert!*"

Suddenly the voice of a disc jockey was raving back at him, and their voices went on rising hysterically together, until Corder let go a deafening scream, trying to drown out the sound. Again and again he screamed, deafeningly, crazily, trying to smash the other voice into silence.

At three o'clock she couldn't stand the hotel room any longer.

She took off her caftan, which was made of dark green velveteen, and put on her new midiskirt. It was caught at the front like a Victorian riding habit and gave her the look of a period governess. After she'd changed, she rested a hand on the telephone for a moment, undecided whether to call or not. Instead she left the room and went down to the lobby.

She chose a seat where she could see both the entrance doors and the reception desk. She opened a fashion magazine in her lap and sat there waiting.

After half an hour there was still no sign of him, so she went over to the reception desk. "Has there been a message for me?"

"What name was it, Madame?"

"Mrs. Ferris."

The clerk checked through the letters in the pigeonhole. "I'm sorry," he said.

Louise crossed to the telephone booths opposite. She dialed the Wickham Market number and waited. When he answered, his voice sounded thin, filtered by the distance.

"Colonel Ferris."

"What's happened? Can I speak to you now?"

"Yes, by all means, sweetie. I'm afraid there's been a . . . a bit of a complication."

Louise waited and when he didn't go on she said, "Why didn't you telephone?"

"I was just going to. The fact is, I only just remembered as I was leaving that I'm committed to rather a large dinner party tonight. Can't think how I forgot."

"I see." She knew her voice sounded shrill. She said, "But what about our plans . . . we were going to discuss things. . . ."

"I'm rather afraid they'll have to wait. I really am terribly sorry."

She waited, but he didn't go on. "Well . . ." She said it uncertainly. She was aware of feeling exhausted.

"I'll be in touch . . . don't worry," he said crisply. "And I really am sorry."

She put the receiver carefully back in the cradle. Then she went over to the reception desk again to ask for her bill.

As Ferris replaced the receiver, Stella Ferris, who was sitting in the window seat across from him, said, "I'm sometimes worried by the ease with which you lie." She took a cigarette from the monogramed box on the table beside her, fitted it carefully between her lips, and waited. The Colonel crossed the room to her and flicked his lighter.

She leaned back, watching him as he returned to his chair by the telephone. "Anyway," she said, "you dealt

183

with her rather well. The trouble with seducing the wives of tradesmen is that they get above themselves. Did she *really* think you were going to take her away from all that drudgery. . . ."

Ferris crossed his long legs. "One imagines so."

"And they're so *impractical!* She can't possibly have believed that your pension is enough to live on."

Ferris crossed his legs. "For Christ's sake," he said irritably, "I've given her the chop. There's no need to go on about it."

Through a drift of smoke Stella Ferris watched him without pity. "If you want to behave like a tomcat I suggest you go down to Brighton or somewhere, where you're not known and, more important, where I'm not known. Let's have luncheon somewhere out."

"All right." Ferris raised his eyes to her at last.

"We could go down to Orford and have lots of lovely oysters."

Ferris stood up. "What about young Michael. . . ."

"Not Michael," she said, "that would be a bore." She crushed out her cigarette in a filigree silver dish. "I daresay he can amuse himself. As a family that seems to be our forte, doesn't it?"

Later, as they went down the steps, Colonel Ferris had recovered his good humor. He touched his moustache lightly with a knuckle. "Whose car shall we take . . . yours or mine?"

"Darling, do let's be accurate . . . they're both mine." Then with a smile she added, "But we'll take the one you usually drive."

And when they were driving through the pine forest toward the coast, Stella said, "I hope you didn't borrow

all her savings . . . the way you did with that last poor
girl."

"Of course not, darling."

"I often wonder what dreadful thing it was your
mother did to you that you've been fleecing women ever
since."

Louise walked without volition, carried along by the
Saturday crowd. In her heart she'd known that Ferris
wouldn't make it. They were both imprisoned by their
marriages, but Ferris lacked the will to escape.

Halfway along Oxford Street she came to a theater
showing an old Bergman film, and she bought a ticket
and went in. She had been sitting in the darkness for only
a few minutes when a man slipped quietly into the seat
beside her. A moment later he was offering her a cigarette.
She stood up without answering and walked toward the
exit.

Outside in the street two nuns were leaving a taxi-
cab. She reached it just in time. "Liverpool Street Station,"
she told the driver.

[3]

"Why don't you kill me now, Fleming . . . why don't you blow the bloody place up!"

"Please, Corder. . . ."

"In fact why didn't you do it first thing. Maybe it's because you're finding it enjoyable."

Denis was sitting at the piano, holding his palms together, looking across at the intercom. "I've told you already, Corder. . . . It would have been cruel to have ended your life without you ever knowing why. You're not a pheasant. You have a conscience." Denis lowered his hands to the yellow keys of the piano.

The soft experimental music which Corder had interrupted began again. Fleming was playing, from memory, "Brother James's Air," and having slight difficulty with the phrasing. "He leadeth me," he murmured under his breath, "He leadeth me the quiet waters by." The dissonance echoed sharply against the window.

The piano had been in the house when they bought it and not worth the cost of removal. Once, long ago, he'd had a piano tuner look at it, but the frame was wooden and the strings wouldn't hold their tension. Denis stopped for a moment and wiped the tips of his fingers on his handkerchief. He spread his hands again but, in the act of playing, stopped.

"I used to play at Saxtead Church on alternate Sundays when I was young. You didn't know that, Corder. . . ." He waited, but Corder didn't answer.

"What are you doing, Corder?" He waited again before saying, "Louise made me give it up. She said she didn't care for the image . . . whatever *that* meant. Corder, why don't you answer?"

Denis brought his fingers gently down on the keys again, playing the "Nunc Dimittis." "Well, I suppose I do know what she meant really . . . I composed a voluntary once."

They'd sung the "Nunc Dimittis" not only after the second lesson but also at the end of Evensong as the choir slowly wound their way back to the vestry in the dim light. It had been a pleasing innovation which he, Denis, had suggested to the vicar. He chanted the words now in a thin, reedy voice.

"Lord, now lettest thou thy servant depart in peace: according to thy word.

"For mine eyes have seen: thy salvation:

"Which thou hast prepared: before the face of all people."

His hands went on mechanically through the stanzas, but he stopped singing. He'd forgotten the church, and was thinking of Corder. Corder would not depart in peace, Corder would depart in terror. Denis closed his eyes and saw there a kind of dark redness, an imagined reflection from the awful holocaust to come. He opened his eyes again quickly. He'd read somewhere that people suffocated quickly from the lack of oxygen created by the flames.

They hardly ever felt the pain of burning.

Corder had been back across the bridge four times and was getting almost blasé about it. He now had six floorboards stacked close to the railing on the landing. The stairs were in a dogleg down into the living room and on the halfway landing he'd already laid two drawers on their ends. They came to just a few inches above the height of the railing. He'd been able to swing these out on the end of a plank, over the air space, and thus avoid the photoelectric switches which he knew were on the first flight of stairs.

Before leaving the bedroom he'd torn a sheet into strips and wound it around his waist where it was out of the way. *If* he ever got downstairs and there was some way of making bridges there, he might have to tie planks together. The whole of the downstairs floor was sensitive, Fleming had said, and it lay underneath his bedroom with much the same dimensions.

Corder laid all his planks down to the drawers on the lower landing, putting one on top of the other. It sloped steeply and he doubted if he'd ever be able to get back again. He sat there crouched on the first set of drawers,

making sure in his mind that there was nothing else he
could make use of. His eyes hurt, probably with sweat, and
the strips of sheet around his middle were already dirty
from crawling. He wiped his face, turned his head watch-
fully to the intercom.

Although he'd paid little attention to it, he was grate-
ful for the terrible piano recital Fleming had given him.
He didn't want Fleming to know he could get downstairs.
And once downstairs he'd thought of a possible way to get
out. It was essential to deceive Fleming till the last moment, and not to provoke him in any way, because he was
now certain of Fleming's mental breakdown. Fleming's
conversation had a rambling quality, and although he
asked continually what Corder was doing, his concentration was so poor that he hardly ever waited long enough
for an answer. He was quite capable, Corder thought, of
breaking the circuit in a moment of pique.

Corder took several deep breaths and started to
clamber onto the planks. Because there were several of
them, there was no sag this time, and he crawled down
steadily until he reached the lower buttress. Then he
balanced himself on one of the drawers and started to lift
the planks away and stack them behind him against the
railing, running up into the air space above the landing.
He could now see the living room with the front door at
the far end on the left. His rod was in the umbrella stand
beside it and his coat and gun were hanging from the
hooks. Then, next to the door on the other side and almost
level with the top of it, he saw the picture rail which
he hadn't particularly noticed before. It ran around most
of the room. It was old-fashioned and strong-looking, but
would it bear one end of his bridge? He brushed his face
with a hand. He imagined the plunge if the rail wasn't

strong enough. And after that the sudden roaring con-
flagration.

The span was nearly twelve feet, and longer than any
of the planks, so he began the awkward business of bind-
ing two of them together. First they had to be positioned
in his lap, projecting both ways into the room toward the
window and toward the fireplace, because of their length.
Then it required all his weight to hold them there while
he wound the bandage around them.

When they were firmly knotted together he maneu-
vered them slowly in the direction of the door. Squatting
on the drawers he couldn't get enough traction to balance
the weight of the double plank, so he lowered his feet carefully to the landing itself, and braced his knees against
the rails.

"Corder, what are you doing?" And then, after a
silence, "Are you praying? That would be the most useful
thing. Have I told you about the prayers we had at school,
Corder? We always assembled at chapel before lessons
and. . . ."

Fleming's regression, he'd noticed, seemed to be going
further and further back. He tried to close his mind
against Fleming's voice as he slowly swung the planks out
toward the far wall. His muscles ached with the stress, and
in spite of himself he couldn't stop the far end from dip-
ping dangerously toward the floor. He fought it up slowly,
time and time again, straining to get it above the level of
the picture rail.

He could almost feel the knotting of his stomach
pressed against the rail, as the far end of the planks swayed
up and down only six inches away from the wall. Then
he summoned all his will and almost wildly flung it up
and pushed it the last little bit. In fact it rose only an

inch or two, but it was just enough to reach the edge of the picture rail, where it rested precariously.

Corder slowly lowered his end to rest on the drawers, then sank heavily against the rail himself. The clack of Fleming's voice was going on, but Corder was only conscious of the speed of his heart, a roll almost, on a bass drum. Then the phone began to ring steadily just below him.

Corder could see it on the table by the west window and his eye moved between it and the intercom panel at the bottom of the stairs. It went on and on. Corder closed his eyes.

When it stopped at last, he heard Fleming's voice say, "I wonder who that was. Was my wife expecting you to join her today, Corder? And now she's wondering where you are?" For almost a minute Fleming hummed what sounded like another piece of church music. Then, "Well, as long as you realize there's no point in you trying to get down to the telephone. . . . You really can't put your weight on any part of the ground floor. What are you doing, Corder?"

Corder shoved the planks tight to the opposite wall and leaned over to bounce them lightly with his hand. It looked a dangerously long span and the picture rail wasn't a very stable support for his weight.

"Why don't you answer me? I know you're there!"

Louise left the phone booth outside Woodbridge station and went to sit in the Renault. Her suitcase was on the passenger seat beside her. There had been no reply from the house and when she'd rung the cottage on the off chance that Denis might be there, there had been no reply from there either.

She didn't like returning home without warning Denis first. It was an essential part of their relationship that in the event of a change of plan, one always telephoned. She sat there with her hands in her lap, debating what to do. She could have lunch at The Bull and telephone afterward or she could go straight back now. She started the engine and drove up to Market Square. Then she remembered that it was too early to lunch at The Bull, and she drove on toward the bypass and home.

There was, after all, nowhere else to go.

As Corder eased himself onto the planks, they dipped gently beneath his weight and he heard the far end squeak against the wall. Once clear of the banister, there would be no getting back.

Like the vole, he was paying the price of his immorality. He thought of Fleming sitting out there in the garage waiting for him to run out in a blind panic. Fleming sitting there with sulfur-yellow eyes.

He drew his body forward slowly, moving only inches at a time. The beams on the ceiling barely cleared his back, and below him the carpet pattern looked like the quilted landscape seen from a plane, so that it gave the illusion of flight. As his weight slowly approached the middle where the planks had been bound together, the sag became more pronounced. He watched the end resting on the picture rail bend slowly upward. The boards creaked and seemed to jar slightly.

For a whole minute Corder lay still, hardly daring to blink his eyes. Then he started to move again, this time in quarter inches.

Then Fleming's voice said, "I think I'll go up to the house soon . . . and have some coffee." He went on, speaking much louder. "I'm rather disappointed in you, Corder. I expected you to try and get out. In fact I was certain you'd be dead by now. Corder? Tell me where you are?"

Denis had examined the windows carefully one by one through the field glasses. He was annoyed that Corder was sulking; he really had expected Corder to respond to the technological challenge. After all, he came from America.

But what he'd hoped for even more was Corder's submission.

He'd wanted Corder to confess, and he'd wanted, in his way, to offer forgiveness. It was as important in its way as the necessity to have explained to Corder why he had to die. And Corder shouldn't have called him a pervert. He should never have done that.

"You shouldn't have called me a pervert. It shows you're very ignorant. I . . . I'm not without knowledge, you know, people like me are quite common, really. The complaint is very well documented. I read all about it in the medical section in the Cambridge library. It's only two hours' drive from here . . . I often go there on business. One of the biggest electronic firms in the country has its factory there. In fact, this intercom kit is one of theirs . . . it's rather good, don't you think? Corder?"

Denis moved away, pressing nervously at his moustache. "What were we talking about. . . ." He passed the piano and closed the lid with a bang as he moved. It was something important he had to explain to Corder. . . . Oh yes.

"It comes under the heading of an Oedipal complex, as a matter of fact. The funny thing is it's common mostly among men with wives much younger than themselves . . .

and also among men who are social failures. That's not me, of course . . . that's certainly not me."

Denis leaned against the bench. He was very disappointed in Corder. Corder had seemed so strong, so . . . so aggressive.

"Fortunately, the prognosis is quite favorable . . . one gets over it in the end. It's quite harmless, you know."

Denis clicked on the transistor again, and a chamber orchestra was playing "The Lily of Laguna." He moved down to the intercom panel. He smiled briefly at it, as if it was Corder's face. "I'll go to Matins tomorrow. I usually go to Evensong, but I shan't tomorrow. I'll go to Matins. And I'll pray for your soul, Corder."

Denis moved away. He was walking in time with the music. He was feeling thirsty. He'd pray for Corder's soul.

"Man that is born of woman hath but a short time to live and is as full of . . . sorrow. He cometh up. . . ."

Denis clenched his eyes tight in an effort to remember. "He cometh up and is cut down like a flower . . . like a *flower.*"

He stopped suddenly as if he had met a wall. A wall of reality. Tears had formed in his eyes, and he felt the warmth of them on his cheek.

Corder was three feet from the front door when the crash came.

He'd hardly heard the music or Fleming's mad, rambling talk; his mind was completely obsessed with the rail ahead of him, from which the plank seemed to hang by a fraction of an inch. There was constant movement in the plank, a slight springing every time he moved, but he couldn't look back to check on the other end of the bridge. The first warning he had was a creaking of wood which ended in a crack, and he felt the sudden jolt as the end behind him slipped.

As the planks shivered violently he glanced back. The drawers had given way and the end of the plank had dropped to the banister rail. But what brought Corder's heart to his mouth was the sight of the drawers still swaying. Then, very slowly it seemed, the top one slid away, hit the first stair of the flight, and went bouncing down to skid along the floor.

Corder closed his eyes, expecting death.

Fleming was shouting. "What was that! What are you doing, Corder? Corder, answer me!"

Corder opened his eyes slowly. His face was wet, he realized, and suddenly he had a compulsive desire to urinate.

The drawer was not heavy enough to have set off the underfloor switch, and as it bounced down the stairs it must have been just below the level of the infrared beams.

"Corder? Tell me what that noise was?"

Fleming's breathing sounded very loud over the intercom.

"Please, Corder. . . ."

Corder looked ahead. The end of the plank resting against the picture rail hadn't shifted. His eyes moved across to the front door, and he could see the contact switch quite clearly, the flat spring clip fitted to the frame and gripping the silver lug which Fleming had shown him the other day. And Corder had thought of a way of dealing with it if he ever got near enough. To the left of the door were the iron hooks from which hung his shooting coat and his gun.

He hoped the hooks were firmly fixed. His life depended on it, he thought wryly. He pushed his hands carefully forward again and gripped the edge of the plank. He started to pull his body, very slowly.

"Isn't there something you want to tell me, Corder? I mean isn't there someone I should write to in America afterward. Or is there anything you'd especially like me to do? Please tell me. . . ."

When the time came, he would have to get under the plank somehow and swing on it to get impetus enough to jump for the hooks. But he wouldn't be able to swing too violently or he might dislodge the plank, and that, if it fell, would be heavy enough to set off one of the floor switches. Corder's arms went gently forward again. Distantly he could hear a flight of jets pass somewhere to the south. As the blast of their engines faded, he heard a new sound.

A car was turning up the driveway.

It accelerated gradually, and as it passed by the house Corder screamed, "Help!" with all the power he possessed. "Help!"

The windowpane seemed to rattle with it, but the car drove smoothly on. Corder, listening, recognized the soft exhaust note of the Renault. It was Louise. Louise was back.

"Fleming!" he shouted. "Do you hear? She's come back! And when she finds you're not in the house, she'll come down here. . . . You won't be able to stop her! Now you'll have to kill us both, Fleming!"

Denis was crouched beside the bench, staring out of the window as the Renault climbed away past the screen of buddleia.

"Oh, no," he whispered shakily. "Oh no, oh no . . ."

He started toward the door, collided with the padded chair, stumbled on. Outside, the sunlight seemed to shock him, and he waited, blinking for a moment, before setting off at a run up the drive. He ran jerkily, all elbows and knees, like a marionette.

He should have known she'd come back, he thought wildly. He'd really been very stupid. He should have known she'd come back when Corder didn't turn up.

[4]

Corder had heard the noise in the garage and the slam of the door. He knew Fleming was gone. He was level with the hooks and they were about three feet away to his left. Now he had to get down, beneath the plank without rolling it. He squirmed slowly, sideways, until he was lying across it; then he began to lower himself over the side, little by little, until he was hanging, his feet only inches clear of the floor. He hoped to God there was no vibrator or photoelectric switch on the wall where the hooks were. His shoulders ached as he began to move his body to and fro.

Gently, he thought, for Christ's sake, gently.

When he'd swung as far as he dared, he bunched his body for the leap. He was hardly conscious of moving through the air, just the sudden bone-crunching crash as he hurtled into the wall and clung there, one hand on a coat hook. Quickly he raised himself until he could get an elbow over the hook. Then he hung, heaving for breath.

"Darling?" She went from the bathroom into the bedroom. The bed was unmade, and his pajamas were on the floor. She bent to pick them up automatically and dropped them on the bed.

"Darling. . . . Are you there?" Her voice was faintly troubled. She turned and went downstairs again.

When she went into the living room there were the remains of a meal on a tray beside the wing chair. She touched the coffeepot but it was cold. Then the french window burst open and Denis was facing her.

"Darling!" She started to go forward automatically but stopped.

Denis said, "What are you doing here?"

"I had a splitting head when I woke in the morning, and I decided not to stay after all. What on earth's the matter?" She noticed for the first time that he hadn't shaved and there was dust on his shoulders. "Where have you been?"

"You came back because he wasn't there," said Denis wildly. "I know all about it." He ranged down the room in his jerky way. "I knew this would happen in the end. I always knew that you'd go off with one of them. But I . . . I stopped him, you see." He pressed his moustache for a moment as if checking the words.

Louise sat on the edge of the chair. Suddenly she was frightened. "You stopped *who?*"

"Corder, of course."

"Corder!" She waited. The clock chimed softly, a note of incongruous sanity in the room.

Denis closed his eyes. "Why, oh why . . . did you have to come *back!*" He groaned and turned away.

"What have you done, Denis?"

"Nothing."

"Where's Corder?"

"He's . . . he's at the cottage."

Then Denis was gabbling. "I haven't done anything. . . . On my word of honor. Corder's doing it to himself, you see." He went and sat on the chaise and covered his face with his hands.

"Doing what?"

"I wish you'd leave me alone," he whispered. "Can't you see that I'm under a strain?" With his eyes closed, the darkness was restful. He stayed still. He would have to go back soon. But he would rest like this first, rest his eyes in the darkness. Then he heard the slam of her car door.

He was up and running before the engine caught. As he burst from the front door, the Renault was just moving off, turning in a tight circle. He threw himself across the hood and dimly saw her frightened face before he started to slip away. He tried to claw his way against the centrifugal force, but the next moment he was falling.

The gravel bit into his knees. Then he was on his feet again and chasing her. He leaped for the door this time, and as he caught the handle he felt the whole car heel over. But before he could press the button catch, she had accelerated suddenly.

The pain was blinding as his thumb was dislocated, then he was rolling in the drive again. This time the gravel was like sandpaper on the side of his face and the heels of his hands. He lay there, breathless, watching the Renault as it left the driveway and careered up the bank. It began to overturn, righted itself, and swerved into a flower bed where it stalled in the soft earth.

He heard the engine catch and rev but the car only bucked, sending up a spray of earth as it dug itself in. He got to his feet slowly and went limping up toward it.

Corder's legs ached with the strain of keeping them hauled up clear of the floor. He had moved the gun onto the peg nearest the door and was going through the pockets of his shooting coat with his free hand. There were cartridges in the side pocket and he dropped two of them into the breast pocket of his pajama jacket. It occurred to him that if he ever got out, Fleming might try to kill him some other way. Then he went feverishly through the other pockets of the jacket and found an old screw and a ballpoint pen with a metal cap, either of which looked aˢ if it might fit the spring clip on the door switch.

Where his arm was crooked over the peg the pain started to become excruciating. Very carefully, he hoisted his body so that he could get his other arm over the next peg where the gun was hanging. Then gradually he transferred his weight to the new peg. It was more than a minute before his circulation came back and he could straighten his arm. When he could, he put a hand out to touch the lever of the mortise lock.

"Now, please God . . . *dear* God . . . ," he said out loud. Somewhere in the distance the engine of a car was revving furiously, but his whole being concentrated on the catch. He bent the lever slowly and watched the bolt withdraw. Then he raised his eyes to the spring clip. Ever so gently he started to open the door. The jaws of the spring clip parted a fraction as the tongue withdrew. There was just room, he hoped, to slip the metal ball-point in behind it. His hand left the lock tensely and came back to his pocket in slow motion.

His fingers felt for the pen, and then he was reaching up slowly again. Whatever happened, he mustn't fumble. He fitted the end of the pen cap into place at the back of the clip and then pushed it in. As the jaws of the spring clip opened a little more, the door was released and it creaked open a few inches. Curled in a knot of pain, Corder stared out at the sun-warmed porch. Just one more effort.

Then somewhere outside he heard running footsteps.

Louise tried letting out the clutch slowly and keeping the revs as low as possible. The car jolted, but the wheels wouldn't grip. Then, looking through the rear-view mirror, she saw the fine spray of upflung dirt and beyond it the lumbering figure of Denis as he left the drive and came up toward her. He ran awkwardly, holding one arm with the other, close against his body. She pressed the accelerator flat, in desperation, and the engine screamed. The car veered heavily to one side and settled deeper. With trembling hands she flung open the door and almost fell out onto the soft earth. Then she got to her feet and raced away.

She ran up the hill, making for the buddleia. From behind, she heard Denis shouting. But it was a scream almost, the words indistinguishable. She fought her way through the white, brittle branches and went leaping down the bank toward the driveway and the cottage beyond. As she crossed the driveway, she heard Denis cry again and when she looked back she saw he had fallen and was lying twisted at the bottom of the bank. He lifted a shaking arm into the air, still shouting words she couldn't hear.

She was laboring for breath herself as she fought for a moment with the catch of the wicket gate, then she fled on again up the path through the rose bed. The front door was open, she noticed. In the next moment she saw the half-naked, contorted figure and as she checked involuntarily, Corder was shouting at her, "Stop! Get back! Don't come near, for Christ's sake . . ."

He was pressed to the wall, dirty, unshaven, and with his pajamas in shreds.

What's happening?" Her voice was only a terrified croak, and in spite of herself she went another two steps.

Corder's voice rose desperately. "Stay there! Stay there, or you'll blow the whole bloody place up!"

She moved away a step, clamping a wrist against her mouth to hold back a scream. Corder watched her go, his body bunched, his feet pressing the wall. Then he leaped.

He fell with a crash clear of the threshold and rolled on the floor of the porch, scattering empty flowerpots. For a moment he lay there shaking, and as he climbed unsteadily to his feet he heard Fleming calling his name. "Corder!"

He leaned back in the doorway, grabbed the gun from the hook, and snapped it open. As he fumbled the cartridges from his breast pocket, Louise's terrified face was pushing against his shoulder.

"Please!" she wailed shrilly. "Please stop it! What's happening . . . ?"

Then beyond her, like an echo, Fleming shouted, "Corder, wait. . . ."

Denis had taken a shortcut from the gate and was charging blindly across the rose bed. He could see Louise standing there, rigid with fear. Just beyond her, Corder was slamming the breach of a gun and twisting it into his shoulder.

"No, Corder! Don't be a fool. . . ."

The words were lost in a flashing roar, and Denis felt a blow in his stomach. He tried to take another step but somehow he was down on one knee. He was vaguely conscious of a great chorus of rooks blended with intolerable pain.

"You don't understand, Corder," he whispered. "I . . ." Then he was on his back, and he could see his spectacles swinging gently from a stem just above his head. He wanted to press his moustache, but he wasn't quite certain where his hand was.

Louise said sickly, "You've killed him . . . you've murdered him." She wanted to move there, to Denis's side, but her legs seemed rooted where they were. "Why have you. . . ."

"Because he was mad," said Corder quietly. "He was going to kill us all. In another moment he'd have been through that door or smashed a window or something. Don't you understand. . . . He's got the house wired to blow it up! With me inside! That's what he was doing a couple of weeks ago."

But Louise was moving stiffly away at last, toward Denis. Corder broke the gun automatically and, stepping back into the porch, extracted the other shell with difficulty.

There wasn't much blood, just a few spots at the top of his fly. As she knelt beside him in the earth she noticed that his eyes were open but unfocused. She whispered, "Denis?" And as if it might somehow help him to speak, she took the spectacles off the rose branch and hooked them back on his nose.

But he stayed motionless. Louise got to her feet and started running down to the wicket gate and up the driveway. Corder watched her go. He had a sudden bout of nausea and turned away, but he wasn't sick. He moved to stand over Fleming.

"I'm sorry, Fleming," he said in a shaking voice.

One of Fleming's legs was twisted. Corder knelt where Louise had knelt and took the leg carefully in his hand. As he tried to move it, Fleming's sudden shriek froze him in the act. He saw Fleming's eyes flutter.

Then in an unexpectedly clear voice Fleming said, "I couldn't really have done it. I realized that this morning. But I wanted Corder to . . . to . . ."

"Fleming?" Corder waited, but no more words came. He sat back on his heels, feeling the sun warm on his back. In spite of it, he was shivering.

After an age he heard a bell clamoring insistently, somewhere in the distance.

"The blood is terribly good for the roses. That's why they have such marvelous roses in hospital gardens. "

"We know that, Mrs. Fleming, but we'd just like you to stay here until the doctor's through." The Inspector was quite young and wore, unexpectedly, casual clothes which looked expensive.

"Of course I'll wait," said Louise clearly. "You've no

need to worry." Then she laughed and added, "I'm all right, you know. You can leave me now."

Beyond the Inspector she could see a uniformed man helping Corder into the back of one of the police cars. Corder was wearing a police raincoat over his pajamas. There was another police car beyond that, with its roof light flashing blue.

Inspector Webb left Louise sitting on the running board of the Land-Rover and went back to where the doctor still knelt beside Denis Fleming's body. His trousers were cut away and the doctor had just withdrawn a bloody finger from Fleming's rectum.

"The bowel's perforated," he said quietly. "Where the hell is the ambulance?"

"It's on its way. . . . It should be here any moment."

As he covered Denis with a blanket, the doctor said, "Get through to Ipswich and tell them they'll need theater staff for a major abdominal. As soon as possible."

The Inspector said, "Right."

"Where's Mrs. Fleming . . ."

"She's over there. By the Land-Rover."

Corder sat in the back of the police car, which smelled strongly of stale cigarette smoke.

In spite of the coat a policeman had put around him he felt cold. He'd explained briefly to the Inspector what had happened and warned him about the gas. The Inspector had been brusque and watchful. "Thank you very much for telling us, sir," was all he had said.

Corder heard an alarm bell nammering, and a moment later an ambulance swung out of the trees and braked just in front of the police car. He saw the crew climb down and open the back. Then they were dashing

off with a stretcher. Corder pressed his cold hands together
and bent his head. He was feeling thirsty and he realized
he'd had nothing to eat or drink since the previous evening.

The ambulance men came back alongside the police
car where the walking was smoother. Corder wound down
the window as they went by. He wanted to see Fleming's
face, to see if Fleming was conscious, but Fleming's head
was turned the other way. The doctor walked behind,
still in shirt sleeves, carrying his bag. A few paces behind
him was Louise.

Corder fluttered a hand at the window, trying to catch
her eye, and she glanced back for a moment, her face
bright and empty.

Corder started to say, "I'm sorry. . . ." But she was
already out of earshot. He watched them load the stretcher,
and there seemed to be a sort of argument before Louise
followed the doctor into the back of the ambulance. It
turned gently and drove away. Corder looked back at the
cottage.

A police sergeant was leaning out of the open bedroom window talking to the Inspector, who was standing
in the garden below. So they'd got inside. Then Corder
saw another policeman carrying his shotgun down to the
second car. He was carrying it carefully with a pencil
through the trigger guard, as if it was contaminated.

Corder said aloud, "Oh, for Christ's sake. . . ." He'd
admitted firing the shot in self-defense.

Another police car arrived soon afterward and the
Inspector asked Corder to move to it.

"Is this going to take long, Inspector?"

"It depends."

"I'd like some clothes. . . ."

"We'll fix you up at the station, sir."

Corder went to the other car and was joined by a policeman and the Inspector in the back. The Inspector sat on a folding seat, facing Corder, as if declaring himself in some way. He had a face which was hard and somehow permanently young. His eyes still had the steady regard of questioning adolescence. The other policeman sat stolidly, his cap balanced on his knee. As they speeded up through the village, a small knot of people parted from the roadway in front of the store.

Corder said, "You got into the house okay?"

"Yes, sir," Webb nodded.

"I suppose I'm lucky to be alive." Corder was irritated that his voice wavered slightly. He half-smiled, and the Inspector smiled back noncommittally.

"He was crazy, of course. And in a way that made it tougher. I was never quite sure when he would take it into his head to blow the place up. I don't mind admitting I was scared stiff. He'd been setting it up for a long time, of course. . . ."

Inspector Webb was looking away out the side window.

"You do *want* me to tell you about it, Inspector?"

"Not at the moment, sir, if you don't mind. It's better to wait until we get to the station where we can get a written statement."

Corder leaned back, holding the coat close about him. After a while, when they were on the road through Wickham Market, Inspector Webb said, "Was that your Land-Rover by the garage, sir?"

"Yes. I bought it from a used-car place in Woodbridge when I first came down."

"My brother-in-law has one. He is very pleased with his."

The ambulance accelerated when it reached the main road, and the driver was operating the alarm bell whenever he passed another car. The doctor was crouched beside the stretcher, holding the dressings under the blanket. Louise stood above him, clutching the ceiling rail and swaying with the motion.

"I wasn't going away with him, darling. As a matter of fact, I liked him least and. . . ."

"He can't hear you, Mrs. Fleming."

"I wanted to go on as we were. I didn't mind. When you're better we'll move. Nearer Margaret and the others. . . ."

Denis's face was yellow against the sheet, and the doctor felt sudden warmth beneath his hand.

As he reached for Denis's wrist the ambulance was pulling into the emergency entrance.

After Corder had made his statement, the policewoman closed her notebook and Webb said, "Get it typed up right away."

"Yes, sir."

Corder had changed into a sweater and blue uniform trousers, which they'd given him.

Through the window there was a builder's yard, and two men went to and fro carrying fresh pine planks.

Inspector Webb said, "She shouldn't be long, sir, then you can sign it. I'd like you to wait through here if you don't mind." He opened another door into a soulless corridor and Corder walked in, still holding his pajamas in a bundle. The Inspector opened a heavy, barred door into a small room with a bunk bed.

Corder stopped on the threshold. "What's going on?"

"I'm sorry it's not more comfortable, but we'd like you to stay here until the statement's typed and our inquiries are complete."

"But why do I have to stay *here?* Why can't I go home?"

Webb waited with the door open.

"Because there may be charges, sir. We've just had the hospital on the phone and Mr. Fleming was dead on arrival."

"But *he* was trying to kill *me*," said Corder violently.

"I think I should tell you, sir, that there was no gas in the cellar, nor was there any means of igniting it if there had been."

Corder shook his head slowly. "But I smelled it! I smelled it on the landing!"

"The pilot light in the boiler was out, that's all you smelled. It can happen with those old boilers." Webb closed the door gently, without haste.

"But you've seen the house. You know what he was trying to do!"

"I've seen the house, yes, sir. But we only have your word as to what he was trying to do. . . ."

"But you saw the burglar alarm . . . and the rest of it. . . ."

"It's not a crime to fit a burglar alarm, sir. What I'm trying to say is this, sir, that the evidence points in both directions. If you intended to kill the deceased, then you could have been constructing an alibi for yourself in advance."

"But why should I want to kill him?"

"I don't know, sir. We've yet to take a statement from Mrs. Fleming."

Corder almost sobbed. "You're crazy, Inspector."

"You said that about Mr. Fleming, sir. I assure you we're not all crazy."

Corder took hold of the bars and shook them. "This whole thing is plain bloody crazy. . . ."

"Now, now, sir. You're a strong man, I grant you, but you can't break that door down."

Corder saw that the Inspector was pleased to have him behind bars, that he had a small boy's pleasure in a captive animal.

"I'll just see how they're getting on with the statement. . . ."

After Webb had gone, Corder moved to the window, which was also barred. The sky was red beyond it, and somewhere at the top of a tree a blackbird was singing out its heart to the evening. He pushed his cheek against the bars, his eyes searching for it.

He couldn't even see a tree.